Why Do Good Guys Love Bad Girls?

A Man's Guide to Finding a Good Woman

By: Devon Wilfoung

ISBN: 9798677398407

Book Production: Crystell Publications
You're The Publisher, We're Your Legs
We Help You Self Publish Your Book

BOP E-mail ONLY – cleva@crystalstell.com
E-Mail – minkassitant@yahoo.com
Website: www.crystellpublications.com
(405) 414-3991

Printed in the USA

CHAPTER 1

Tyler waited in the living room for his girlfriend, Nesha. It was 5 o'clock in the morning, and she was a no-show. Just when he went to get their son, Tyler Jr., and head to the police station to fill out a missing person report, the door swung open, the wind blew, and in walked Nesha. Wobbly and drunk.

"Oh, God!" Tyler rushed to her aid, "Where have you been?"

Nesha clucked her teeth in annoyance. "Don't be asking where I've been, you fucking lame. Where is my son?" she questioned.

"Upstairs in his baby crib," Tyler said.

"Why you not up there with him?" She headed up the steps of their apartment, with Tyler right on her heels.

"I was worried about you."

She spat. "That's your problem. Always worried about me when you supposed to be worried about our son. Hey, stink'em boo." She picked Tyler Jr. up and gave him a kiss. "Don't wake him up," Tyler told her.

"Shut up." She rolled her eyes at him.

"Where you been?"

"Don't start this shit tonight."

"Then when is a good time to get at you, being that you ain't never at home," Tyler asked.

"When you start making some real fucking money and take care of this family like you should, then you can question me. Until then shut the fuck up!"

A real slap for his ego. "I do the best I can."

"Well, your best ain't good enough. I don't know why I'm still with your UPS-delivering ass!"

"Why are you then?" he challenged.

"Cause I'm just as stupid as you are." She placed Tyler Jr. in his arms. "Hold him while I go and wash up."

***

"You're a chump. You need to put your foot down. Choke some sense into that heffa, and show her who is the boss, either that or she will run all over you," Key told his best friend Tyler.

Tyler let out a deep sigh. "I can't do the mother of my child like that."

"You need to do something cause that hoe out of line," Key banged the table they were sitting at with his fist.

"Calm down," Tyler said silently, looking around and noticing everyone staring at them, "Now I know what it's like to be in the spotlight. Think anyone heard you?" Tyler asked.

"No time for humor. What you need to do is lay down the laws in which govern your household. If you don't stand for something, you're bound to stand for anything," Key stated.

***

Tyler pulled into the parking lot of the three-bedroom apartment he and Nesha shared and thought for a moment: Maybe Key was right! Maybe I did need to lay down the laws that governed my home. He found it ludicrous that he worked damn hard to provide for his family, and all Nesha did was bitch and complain and stay out all night.

He was fed up. He got out of his black 2017 Ford Taurus and stormed into the house. "We need to talk," he said with authority.

"I'm telling you right now! You better lower your tone. Can't you see I'm watching 'Love in Hip Hop'? You know I don't play that." She cut her eyes at him.

Tyler took the remote out of her hand and flicked off the TV. "Right now."

"Cracker, you done lost your dog-gone mind." She roused to her feet.

"I thought so," Tyler said before he heard a clack and felt a stinging sensation. That's when it dawned on him that Nesha had smacked the dog shit out of him.

"Let me tell you one damn thing. You don't run shit up in this house. Let me see the remote." She snatched the TV remote from him.

Tyler rubbed his sore face, "We need to talk," he said more sensibly.

She huffed. "What. What the hell do you want!"

"Just to talk."

She cut the TV back on. "Wait until the show goes off."

"I'm hungry," he told her.

"Then go fix yourself something to eat. Kitchen is wide the fuck open," she smirked.

"Oh, it's like that?"

"Exactly," she remarked.

"I'm tired of this shit."

"Get the fuck out then. Me and my baby don't need you," she went off, raddling her neck back and forth like only a sister can do, "Where you been at anyway? You got off work two hours ago. If I find out you've been messing around on me, Ima do something to you."

"I wasn't around no other girls. I was out with Key," he yelled from the kitchen.

"Umm!" She sucked her teeth. She noticed every time he hung with Key he tried to get buck.

She blurted out, "I don't like him."

"He's my best friend. What you want me to do about it?"

He was right. There was nothing she could do about it, so she left it alone for the time being. She still didn't like Key: he was a bad influence on her man. She didn't need him corrupting her man or giving him any fancy ideals.

Tyler searched for something to eat in the fridge. "Why haven't you been grocery shopping?" he asked.

"I haven't had time. It's some bologna and cheese in there," she shouted from the living room.

"A damn shame a man had to work 12-hour shifts and come home to a freaking bologna sandwich. Shit just didn't get any better than this," he thought out loud, but not too loud that Nesha could hear him. He fixed a sandwich, grabbed a coke and went back into the living room with Nesha. He popped his soda open and sat down quietly until "Love of Hip Hop" went off. "Can we talk now?"

"Yeah. What is it that's so damn important that you had interrupted me in the middle of my favorite program?" She clocked her head to the side and gave him her undivided attention.

"Well, how can I say this," he stroked his beard with the palm of his hand, a habit he had adapted when trying to express his feelings to Nesha.

She smirked. She knew Tyler was powerless when it came to standing up to her. That's one of the reasons she ran all over him.

"Well, I was thinking…"

"Just say it, but hold on because the phone is ringing." She hopped up from her seat. "Let it ring," he said to her.

"It might be important." She ran to the phone.

Tyler watched Nesha prance to the cordless phone and pick up. Even when he was mad at her, she still managed to look immaculate. Nesha had a body most women could only hope for. Nice firm breasts, thick thighs, hips, and ass for days. She resembled the actress Kerry Washington. All the thinking about her great attributes aroused him. He started thinking about the last time they had sex. It had been a minute, two weeks. Nah. Four, to be exact. He went over to where Nesha was at and started kissing on her neck. Then began to rub a path from her breasts down to her vagina.

She shoved him away, "Stop!"

"Who is that girl?" Pamela asked Nesha.

"My baby daddy. He tryna get some," she laughed. "But he knows he's not getting any because I'm about to out with you, and he going to be keeping Tyler Jr.," she claimed.

Hearing all this had Tyler furious. He held in his anger until Nesha got off the phone. "When the fuck were you going ask me if you could go out?" he snapped.

"I don't have to ask you shit. It is what it is. If I want to go out, then that's what I'll do!" she yapped. "You aren't going anywhere," he put his foot down.

Nesha smacked the shit out of him, Bop! "I'm tired of you acting like a hoe! Go watch Tyler while I get dressed."

Tyler watched Nesha walk off. He felt that if going out was more important to her than her own family, then so be it. At this point the only thing that mattered to him in this world was his son, Tyler Jr.

CHAPTER 2

Anthony B looked around the club, and who did he see? His girl Neatra with her cousin Tamra, who was on stage, competing in the Back That Ass Up contest. She was pretty damn good cause she had won the competition hands down. Out of all the clubs in the world, why did his girl have to be in this one, he asked himself. He was about to head out of the club unnoticed when the DJ announced the club was closed. As he headed out he felt someone take his arm. He looked back, and it was this chick that he had been wanting to bone.

"What's good, Kimbella."

She smiled at him from ear to ear. "You," she replied. "I wanted to see what's up with you."

Before he could get two words out, Neatra appeared out of nowhere. Attached to her was Tamra, the winner of the Back That Ass Up contest.

"Who is this bitch!" Neatra shoved the girl glued to Anthony B. "What the fuck are you doing all hugged up with this bitch?" she glared at Anthony B sideways.

"Who are you calling a bitch, hoe?" Kimbella asked.

"You," Neatra retorted.

Before Anthony B knew it, all hell had broken out. Tamra and Neatra had jumped poor Kimbella. It was a lose-lose situation from the start. Anthony B tried his best to break up the double team, to no avail. Once he got either Tamra or Neatra off of Kimbella, the one that was free would bank her.

They didn't stop until police showed up on the scene. And by then everyone took off running. Anthony B hurried to his Lexus 330, climbed in and pulled off. The screeching of the tires was the only thing that you could hear.

He couldn't wait until Neatra got home so he could give her an earful. He pulled into their four-bedroom home in Durham, NC. Soon as he got into the driveway good, his cell went off. There was a text.

We dragged that bitch. At the end: Lol.

These got to be the dumbest broads alive, Anthony B reflected over what had just happened. Afterwards, he called Neatra up.

She answered on the first ring, "What?"

"Bring your dumb ass home."

"What?" She looked over at Tamra. "I know you didn't call me dumb."

"I know he didn't," Tamra added her two cents.

"I'm on the way," she hung up.

***

"You want me to take you home?" Tamra asked Neatra.

"No," she smirked, "I just told him that. You know the Waffle House is popping."

"Which one you want to go to?"

"The one off of T.W. Alexander," Neatra stated.

"You ain't scared Anthony B going to kick that ass?" Tamra asked.

"Picture that," Neatra replied. "Girl, I got that nigga trained. I'm the dog trainer." But in the back of her mind, she knew Anthony B was nothing to play with. "Fuck him," Neatra declared.

"I hear you." And when he beat your ass don't come crying to me. Damn. Anthony B treated Neatra like a queen. And in return, she treated him with no respect. Damn. Why did Neatra have all the luck? Here she was boasting.

Tamra could remember a time when Neatra was in the same predicament that she herself was in. Broke, and down on her luck. That's until Anthony B had walked into Neatra's life and took her ghetto ass out of the hood. Tamra wished she was Anthony B's lady and not the other way around. Real talk. The whole time she was whopping Kimbella's ass, she was doing it for herself and not for Neatra. In all actuality, she felt like Anthony B was too much for Neatra but right up her alley. She could tame him, plus she was his type of chick: hustler wife material; traffic his drugs and all that. On the other hand, Neatra wasn't doing shit but spending all of his money, sitting around the house and doing nothing. And, hell, that tramp was even sleeping around on Anthony B. The nerve of some bitches. Don't worry, bitch. When you fuck up, I'll take up the slack. I'll be the shoulder he can cry on when he finds out you playing him for some local corner hustlers. A waste of time, if you asked Tamra. You could take a bitch out the hood, but you couldn't take the hood out of a bitch like Neatra, Tamra thought as she got off the highway and headed to the Waffle House.

I'ma kill this bitch, Anthony B promised. He had been calling Neatra only to keep getting her voicemail. This girl thinks she got all the damn sense. What she's going to do is make me wring her damn neck. Just as he contemplated, he saw headlights in the driveway.

Neatra stumbled into the house, feeling tipsy. She saw Anthony B on the couch. "Where the fuck you been?" he questioned.

"Me and Tamra went to the Waffle House."

"It's five o'clock in the morning. You told me you would be home three hours ago," he glanced down at his Rolex watch.

"We must've lost track of the time. Let's go upstairs," she commented.

"You full of shit. I ain't no dummy," he scolded.

"What are you talking about?" she played innocent. In all actualities, she and Tamra had been hanging out at the liquor house.

"Just get off of me," he told her as she tried to embrace him. "I don't know why you keep trying to make this work," he said as he shoved her to the side.

"Where do you think you're going?" she questioned. "You're not going anywhere."

"I'm out," he assured her.

"Every time we get into a dispute you wanna run off to one of your bitches' cribs," she caught up with him and got all up in his face.

"Move," he said as he stepped to the side.

"You not leaving here," she shouted.

He smirked and slid her out of the way. "Move."

She knocked his hands away, "Don't you be touching me."

"Then get out of my way," he told her as he headed to the door.

Boom! She hurled her cell phone at him and missed.

"Stupid hoe."

"I got your stupid hoe," she picked up a medal statue of African art and threw it as hard as she could at him.

Anthony B ducked just in time to see Kunta Kinte flying over his head and crash into the wall. "Bitch, is you crazy!" he barked.

"I got your crazy!" She started throwing all kinds of shit. Her Louis Vuitton handbag, pillows, pictures and etc. Too much to name.

Anthony B made a dash for it. He made it to his vehicle safely, got in and slammed the car door shut, just when he thought he got away. He heard a loud bang against the windshield.

"Get your ass out," Neatra hollered.

"Fuck you. It's over." He cranked up his Lexus and stomped on the gas.

***

"No. Oh God," Neatra flopped on the ground as she watched Anthony B pull off. She sobbed, sniffled, and asked herself a question: What should I do? One thought came to mind and that was to call the police. So that's what she did.

"Hello. 911?" she sobbed.

"Whom am I talking to, and what is your reason for calling?" the dispatcher asked.

She thought of a lie. She couldn't lose Anthony B; there was no way, no how. He was the best thing that had happened to her since welfare cheese and food stamps.

"He just put his hands on me," she lied.

"Are you alright?" the concerned dispatcher asked.

She thought for a moment. What if Anthony B left her? What type of predicament would she be in then? "No, I'm not alright. He's leaving."

"Where is he going?"

She thought about the question that was asked. "I don't know," she cried out. But she hoped it wasn't over to another girl's house.

"Do you know what kind of car he's driving?" "No. I'm not no snitch. He's getting away."

"What do you want us to do?" the dispatcher commented. "The only way we can help you is if you tell us what type of car he is driving."

She wasn't no snitch, but she needed her man back desperately. "In a black Lexus GS 360."

"Which way was he going?"

"I don't know. But I do know his license plate number."

"Hold on. Let me get a pen. What is it?" The dispatcher couldn't take down the information fast enough.

***

Anthony B was about to pull into his mother's driveway on Trinity Avenue when, all of a sudden, the police pulled up out of the wood works.

"Get out with your hands up," one officer screamed out.

Anthony B did what the officer demanded. "Excuse me.

What did I do?" he wanted to know as they pulled him out of his vehicle and laid him face down on the ground.

"Shut up, woman beater," the arresting officer commented, placing his foot on the back of Anthony B's neck and spitting a big glob of tobacco onto him. "You like hitting women? See how tough you are when you get up to the big house." The officer snatched Anthony B up roughly, and then he and the crew took turns beating him like a punching bag.

By the time they got finished with him, Anthony had a different type of respect for women.

"Where are we going?" he uttered from the backseat, eyes half shut, ribs sore, if not broken.

"To see if you're the one that's been beating on this sweet lady," the fat cop chuckled in the passenger side of the cop car, hitting his baton against his hand repeatedly.

"There has to be some type of misunderstanding," Anthony B moaned.

"Yeah, right. Sure. We'll see. Pull over right here," the fat cop said to his partner in crime. "You better hope like hell she doesn't know you," the cop laughed. He got out and tapped on the door of the house they were in front of.

Anthony B couldn't make out where he was at. All he could remember before passing out was hearing Neatra telling them that she knew him.

"Bring him in the house," Neatra yelled. "I want him home."

"So he can beat you again?" the cop shouted.

"But he didn't hit me." She tried to open the cop car to get her man free.

"Yeah, right," the cop laughed. "If you want to see your man, then you're going to have to pick him up from the station in 48 hours," he pried her way from the vehicle before they left.

***

The first thing Neatra did was call up Tamra.

***

Tamra woke up from the pounding of the phone. She wasn't in the mood for this right now, she thought as she picked up the phone. "What?" she peered into the phone.

"It's me," Neatra said.

"Girl, what is it. What you doing calling my phone this late in the damn morning for? It better be good." She sat up in her bed.

"Anthony B just got arrested," Neatra told Tamra.

"Slow down, breathe. Now, what happened?" Tamra asked. "What did he get arrested for?"

After listening to the stupid shit Neatra had done, she could only smirk. This stupid bitch. Didn't she know that you were never supposed to call the boys in blue on your man? No man, no matter the circumstance. That's rule number 101 in being a hustler's wife. "What made you call the police?" she held in her laughter. I can't wait to show you how to hold down a real man like the one you just fucked up with, Tamra laughed out.

"I know you're not laughing," Neatra paused.

"No. I'm laughing at the shit you just did. You're crazy, girl," And crazy is as crazy does, she thought.

'I know," Neatra admitted. She rubbed her head. "What am I going to do?" she asked Tamra for her advice.

"Tamra responded with a deep sigh, "I don't know. He's not

going to want to talk to you anytime soon."

"I know." This time it was Neatra letting out a deep sigh. "I can't believe they locked him up. It's not like I pressed any charges."

"Girl, don't you know that the state will take charges out if you don't? Where have you been?"

"I don't know," Neatra said honestly. "I don't want to lose him."

"You do some stupid stuff. You know how many women would love to have a brother like Anthony B?" And she was one of them. She didn't see what Anthony B saw in Neatra besides an okay face and big ass. She never could figure that one out. Neatra was pretty but had nothing on her.

Tamra had a body to die for and a face of grace. She resembled an African queen. Slim waist, nice hips, plump butt, and caramel skin tone. Not bad for her 5 foot 7, 140-pound frame.

Neatra huffed and let out a deep breath. "Yes. I know how many women want Anthony B, but that's too bad cause he's my man, and I'm going to get him back no matter what,"

"What are you going to do?" Tamra wanted to know.

"I don't know. I'll think of something."

"Well, you do that and call me tomorrow," Tamra told Neatra. "I gotta catch up on my beauty sleep."

"Bye, hoe," Neatra hung up.

We'll see who's the hoe when Anthony B leaves your ass, stupid. For me, Tamra snickered.

***

After being locked up for 48 hours, Anthony B was released

from jail with a court date. He couldn't believe Neatra had done this hideous shit. Who did he see as soon as he stepped outside of the court building? Neatra.

"Baby. I'm sorry. I didn't know they were going to lock you up," she tried explaining.

"Taxi," Anthony B motioned for the taxi parked outside of the courthouse.

"Your Lexus got impounded. I got my Mercedes. You don't need a taxi," she said.

"Don't tell me what the fuck I need. Stay the fuck away from me and out my life," he snapped.

"Anthony B. You don't mean that."

"You got me twisted," he said before he hopped into his taxi.

"No. I'm sorry." She tried getting into the taxi.

Anthony B held the door shut. "Get me away from this crazy bitch," he told the driver of the taxi.

"No. Don't go," Neatra screamed out. "I need you," she jiggled the door handle.

Anthony B locked the door, "Go," he told the driver.

"I can't. She's holding onto the door."

Anthony B frowned and gave the driver the look of death. "Step on it," he yelled out. All you could hear was screeching tires.

Anthony B glimpsed back and saw Neatra chasing the taxi. This woman is crazy. He shook his head and took a deep breath, hating the fact that he ever got involved with such a woman in the first place. He should've taken heed when his mom told him Neatra was no good for him. Now he was in too deep.

"Where to?" the driver asked.

Where could he go? He couldn't go home because Neatra

would be there, and he wasn't trying to get locked back up. Cause Lawd only knew that he would probably do Neatra bodily harm. He couldn't go to his mother's house. If she ever found out, she would probably wind up killing Neatra herself. As much as he hated to admit it, deep down inside he still loved Neatra. They just needed some time apart. "To the nearest hotel," he told the taxi. The driver pulled up to the 21c hotel in downtown Durham. Anthony B paid the taxi, got out and purchased a nice room in the executive suite on the top floor. He had a great view that overlooked the entire city. A great place to clear his mind of the crazy shenanigans that had taken place.

CHAPTER 3

Damn. Where is this girl? I'm going to kick her motherfucking ass. I'm tired of this shit. And where the hell is my son? He wanted to know, and someone was about to give him some answers. Why couldn't he come home to a nice cooked meal? Nah. He had to come home to an empty stomach and even emptier home. He was about to go the slam off when he caught up with Nesha.

He got into his Ford Taurus and tried to locate his stupid-ass baby momma. Sometimes he wanted to wring her neck. It was time to earn some respect. l'ma show this woman something, he was saying in the back of his mind. His first stop was Nesha's mom's house. She told him that she hadn't seen Nesha, so he drove over to her Aunt Tracy's place. The same results.

Damn. Where is she? He drove around Durham, UNC Central, Southpoint Mall, even Northgate Mall. He drove by restaurants like Outback and Golden Corral. Nothing. Nothing. He even drove by the Maplewood cemetery, McDougald Projects, the Greyhound bus station, the Amtrak train station, the hood, the boondocks, and still there was no sign of Nesha.

He took a deep sigh. He made a couple of phone calls, and

no one had seen or heard from Nesha.

He called her mother again, "Hello, Ms. Stephens. Have you seen Nesha?"

"I told you I haven't seen her. Can you stop calling my phone?" she told him.

Tyler ended the call. Like mother, like daughter, he thought. Where could she be? He had driven around until 1 o'clock in the morning, looking for Nesha with no luck. He must've checked back home a dozen times. Filled up his gas tank three or four times. He was getting tired. He decided to go by Nesha's friend Pamela's house. He parked and got out of the car, walked to her apartment and knocked.

"Who the fuck is you?" some barbarian asked as he sipped a bottle of Whiskey. "Tyler. Is Pamela here?"

"Who's looking for her?" some other guy answered.

"Me, Tyler."

"Why the fuck you looking for my woman?" the stout guy with the bottle raised an eyebrow.

"I really don't want any problems, big guy," was Tyler's answer.

"Well, you about to have some," the guy popped his knuckles.

Tyler found himself running. Dashing behind building after building, with two angry men on his trail. He wasn't cut out for all this shit. He hopped a fence and must've tripped because he went tumbling and banged his leg up. "Ouch," he bounced back up on his feet.

"He went that way," motioned one of the guys trailing him.

"Damn," Tyler said as he hid behind a house.

"Let's get him. You go this way, and I'll go that way, and

we'll meet up," one coached.

Tyler ran like he was Usain Bolt from the Jamaican track team. The two guys were on him like white on rice, but he outsmarted them. He turned the corner, bust a right, left, left, right, leapt under a porch and hid.

"Where did he go?" one of the guys asked the other.

"I don't know," his pal replied.

"Damn. I was going to kick his ass."

Tyler l stiff in the dirt. He didn't so much as breathe for nearly two minutes until the bad guys departed. That was close. He wiped the sweat from his forehead.

Despite of what happened, Tyler decided it would be best to leave his car and come back for it tomorrow, when the thugs were asleep. Somewhere during the process of running for his damn life, he had lost his cell phone.

Isn't that about a bitch, he confirmed. Where was he going to go? Not back to Pamela's. He had to go somewhere. That somewhere was Nesha's best friend's house. He knocked on the door.

A light came on. "Who is it?"

"Me. Tyler," he answered. He heard the locks on the door being unlatched.

"Tyler? What happened to you?" Amber asked.

"Long story," he responded, dusting off some of the dirt from when he was under the porch, running from those very bad men.

"Come in and tell me what happened," she let him in and looked to see if anyone was behind him. Seeing that the coast was clear, she shut the door back and locked it.

"What happened?" she asked worriedly.

"Don't want to talk about it," he said, ashamed to tell her that

20

he got chased by two men, had to leave his car behind, hid under a porch, laid in the dirt, and all because of her best friend.

"Okay. You don't have to tell me what happened. But you do have to get out of those dirty clothes in my house," she spat.

"Cool. Do you have a bathroom? If so, I can go in and get cleaned up?"

"And get dirt all on my white carpet?" she glared at him. "Get undressed. I won't look," she turned her head and stuck her hand out.

Tyler huffed, got undressed and gave Amber his dirty clothes. Amber took his clothes and glimpsed down at his boxer briefs.

"I'm so embarrassed," he covered himself.

"Don't be." He is stout, she thought before she turned and walked off. "I'll take these clothes and wash them for you."

"Thanks."

"You can take a shower if you want. I have some extra clothes in my closet that might fit you," she said to him.

"Cool. Where is your bathroom?"

"The second door to your right," Amber stated. "The towels and washcloth should be in the closet."

"Cool," he stated, then went into the bathroom and took a long hot shower. He heard a tap on the door and turned around.

"Are you okay in here?" Amber asked.

"Yeah."

"I'm going to step in for a moment and put your clothes on the hamper for you."

"Cool."

Amber stepped into the bathroom. From what she could see through the shower door, Tyler was hung low. In other words, blessed by God. "Do you need anything else?" she commented.

"No. I'm cool."

Too bad, she thought. "Your things are lying on the hamper," she said before leaving.

Tyler wiped the tears from his eyes. He was thinking about his child's mother. Sometimes he loved her. And other times he hated the grief she put him through. Be strong, brother, he told himself before he stepped out of the shower.

"What the fuck is this?" He glimpsed at the attire Amber put on the hamper for him. Without thinking he stepped out of the bathroom naked. "What the fuck is this?" he barked, holding frail gym shorts she had out for him.

Amber covered her mouth, "Tyler," she pointed down at his crotch.

"Oh shit. I'm sorry," he yelled as he went back in the bathroom.

Don't be, Amber thought.

"I didn't mean it," he paced the bathroom floor.

What if she told Nesha? That would be his ass. That was the last thing he needed right now. Nesha would try and kill him.

"Don't worry. It was an honest mistake," she yelled from where she was sitting in the living room.

"I just don't want you to think I tried to come on to you and tell Nesha," he hollered back as his heart pumped at fast pace.

"Calm down. I know you would never do anything intentionally to hurt Nesha." Too bad she couldn't say that about Nesha.

"I have to get home," he told Amber.

"I'll give you a ride once your clothes get dry. And, Tyler, if it means anything to you, I didn't see anything," she lied.

Amber felt sorry for Tyler in ways. She knew he was a good man with a conniving-ass woman. She hated that Nesha took Tyler for granted. Like for real. That girl had so many secrets that Tyler didn't know about. She went in her laundry room and checked the clothes to see if they were ready. While she did so, she took the time to give her girl the heads up.

***

Nesha rolled out of D'angelo's arms and reached for her cell phone.

"Who is that, baby?"

"No one," She told D'angelo. She got out of bed so she could take the call in private and at the same time see what Tyler Jr. was crying about.

"Shut that boy the hell up," D'angelo told her.

"You shut the hell up," she said to D'angelo as she cradled Tyler Jr. in her arms. "Hush, little baby," she said as she answered the call. "Hello."

"Girl, where are you?" Amber scolded.

"At the hotel with D'angelo. "Why?" she asked in response.

"Because while your ass is laid up with D'angelo no-good ass, Tyler is over here worried sick about you."

Nesha panicked, "What is he doing at your house?" she gave Amber the third degree. "Probably looking for you while you lying up with an idiot who don't give a rats ass about you. He just wants some pussy," Amber stated.

"You stay out of my business. I'm grown and I do what I want."

"You need to get home so Tyler can stop worrying about

you," she sympathized for him.

"You need to fall back and let me handle my bitch like I damn near well please. You doing too much," she spat.

"I'm just giving you some friendly advice," Amber said bluntly.

"Don't need it," Nesha let her know.

***

"Neash?" I know this bitch didn't just hang up on me, Amber thought. She checked the dryer to see if Tyler's clothes were ready.

Amber got Tyler's clothes for him and then gave him a ride home. Before he turned to get out of the car, she stopped him. She wanted to tell him about so many things, but she just couldn't right now.

"What is it?" He looked down at her hand on his arm.

"I just wanted to say that you're a damn good man, and I hope you open your eyes soon."

"What's that supposed to mean?" he questioned.

"You'll find out in due time. I just hope that you make the right choices."

"Amber, are you trying to hit on me?" he teased.

"No. I'm just looking out for you, dear friend," she smiled.

"Oh. Cause if you told Nesha what you saw tonight, she would kill me," he chuckled.

"Why are you so scared of her?" she wanted to know.

"Have you ever seen that woman when she is mad and upset?" he joked.

"You have to learn how to stand up for yourself, or else she will run all over you."

"Hey, that's your friend you're talking about," he told Amber.

"Yeah. And you're also my friend." She rubbed his face with the palm of her hand.

"Hey, I better go," he said in a hurry to get out of the car. This shit had to be some kind of setup, he was thinking.

"Bye," Amber waved as she pulled off.

Amber was going to tell about how I walked out of the bathroom butterball naked, he told himself. Me and my stupid ass. He shook his head as he went into the house.

CHAPTER 4

Nesha got out of D'angelo's car with Tyler Jr. in her arms. "See you later."

"Bye," D'angelo replied. He didn't even wait to see if she got into the house safely before he was pulling off.

Nesha joggled Tyler Jr. in her hand as she tried to manage getting her keys out of her purse. Before she could, Tyler opened the door.

"Where the fuck have you been?"

"Hold him," she placed Tyler Jr. in his father's arms. Then she smacked the shit out of him. She yelled, "Are you stupid? Why aren't you at work?"

Tyler rubbed his aching face. "I was worried."

"Worry your ass upstairs and put Tyler Jr. in his baby crib so I can kick that ass," she spat. "For what? I didn't do shit," he tried to explain.

"Go," she gestured. "Your bitch ass. You went by my momma's house. By my aunt's house. My best friend's house," she snapped.

This had to be about Amber, he was thinking. That had to be

the reason she was so upset.

"Nothing happened," he blurted out.

"And nothing ever will happen," she walked up to him and pressed her finger to his skull. "Cause you know if I ever find out that you cheated on me, I'm going to beat your bitch ass," she said. "Now go take him upstairs and bring your ass right back," she gritted her teeth.

"Okay," he said in a defeated voice. He took his son upstairs and placed him into the baby crib.

"It will not always be like this, little man." He rubbed his son's fluffy cheeks and thought about how much he looked like him.

"Tyler. Bring your ass down here," Nesha screamed.

"I am coming," he yelled.

"You better lower your tone when you speak to me," she warned.

He lowered his voice, "I'm sorry."

"You sure got that right. Sorry motherfucker!"

Nesha felt a temper tantrum coming on. First this fool goes to my momma's house. Then my aunt's house. Then over Amber's place. There is no telling what she told him about me, she was contemplating. She waited for Tyler to come downstairs and went to his ass.

She beat him for everything he did the day before. "You had the nerve to go by my momma's house, my aunt's house, by my best friend's place. What in the hell has gotten into you?" she punched him in his head with a closed fist. "Had the nerve to miss work. Got people thinking I'm some kind of tramp that don't come home. Have you lost your mind?"

Tyler covered himself up as Nesha beat him. He wondered

when the beating would stop.

***

Key sat and looked at his best friend Tyler. He felt sorry for him. She just doesn't know what she has. "Some bitches..." he told Tyler at the bar.

"Key."

"Fuck that," Key roared, pounding his fist down onto the table. "I should get some girls around the way to mug that heffa. Look at your face. My girls off of Fayetteville Street would be happy to kick Nesha's ass."

"It's not that bad," Tyler downplayed it.

"Did you catch that number?" Key asked.

"What number?"

"To that truck that hit your face. You always protecting that grimy chick," Key frowned. "I wish you would just let me teach that heffa a lesson one good time."

"Key. Promise you won't."

Key turned his head and looked away. He couldn't bear to look at what Nesha had done to Tyler. He was a good guy. Better man than he was, because if Nesha was tough enough to punch, then she was definitely tough enough to take a punch. He knew Tyler loved Nesha. But the moral of the story was, she was just no fucking good for him.

"Okay," it took everything he could muster not to have his girls from Fayetteville Street pay Nesha a visit. "But under one condition," he told Tyler.

"What's that?" Tyler looked up with his eyes half shut.

Key pulled out a business card, "Give him a call."

"Relationship counselor Mel Brooks," Tyler read from the

card Key gave him.

"Yeah. He's a good friend of mines. He owes me a favor. Just talk to him, and I'll have him set up your first appointment."

"I don't have the money," Tyler said to Key.

"He won't charge you a thing," Key replied. "I seriously think he can help."

Tyler took a deep sigh, "I hope so."

***

"Your honor. My client is innocent. He's never been accused of anything but a few parking tickets. And I understand that Neatra White will not be pressing any charges," Anthony B's lawyer turned his attention on Ms. White.

The judge frowned, "Did he hit you?"

Neatra glanced around the courtroom. Was this a trick question? "No, Your Honor," she replied.

"So you lied?" the judge scolded.

"I wouldn't exactly call it that," she retorted.

"Then what do you call it? Some people call it perjury, which carries a mandatory sentence of at least a year in jail. So think about that the next time you set foot in this courtroom."

Anthony B laughed. The judge turned to him, "I know you men use scare tactics on these women. You may be not guilty. But I'm requiring you to take a relationship course by a specialist that I highly recommend. The price is steep, but that's the price for coming into my courtroom." The judge rammed his gavel.

Anthony B turned to his high-priced lawyer, "I thought you

could beat the case."

"I did. The only thing is, you'll have to finish this class, and this will be sponged from your record."

This girl is costing me too much time and money. Anthony B cut his eyes at Neatra. Sometimes he could kill her.

"How much is this specialist, he's recommending, and when do I start?"

"I'll go get all the information now. Be back in a jiffy," his lawyer said.

"Anthony B, can I talk to you?" Neatra stepped to him.

"Not right now. Go! You the reason I'm in this mess in the first place."

"Anthony B, I'm sorry. I really am," she lowered her gaze.

"Oh yeah. Go tell it to the judge. I don't wanna ever talk to you. You can keep the car. The place. Whatever makes you happy. I'll be by later tonight to get my things."

"You are just talking," she responded. She didn't want to lose him. "Please!"

"Get to stepping and don't look back until you reach your car. I'm long gone, it's over. A wrap," he assured her.

Neatra felt wobbly legged. She felt like she was about to have a seizure or an asthma attack. Couldn't decipher between the two. "No. I love you. Don't leave me," she screamed out as she clutched his shirt. "I need you. Please don't leave me."

"What the fuck!" Anthony B stood to his feet. "She's attacking me. Somebody help," he screamed out.

"Order in court," the bailiff broke up the frenzy. "You go that way. And you go the other," he demanded.

"I didn't do shit," Anthony B spat.

"Come on, tough guy. You like hitting girls? Let's see how

tough you are," the bailiff spat.

"Fellas. Come on," Anthony B's lawyer stepped in between the two men, "What happened?"

Anthony B said, "She attacked me."

"The other way around," the bailiff replied.

Anthony B's lawyer did what was best and hurried his client out of the courtroom. Once out of the courtroom, he said to Anthony B, "You need to put a restraining order on her."

"It'll make me look like a punk."

"Better than a fool," his lawyer warned. "It's the right thing to do."

Anthony B stroked his beard as the bailiff that was talking all that shit in the courtroom escorted Neatra out safely.

"He won't hurt you again," he held her in his arms.

That conniving heffa, he thought. Two could play that game.

***

Neatra waited for Anthony B, wearing nothing but high heels and a thong. To her surprise, the police rolled up in her front yard. At first she thought the Feds or ATF were about to run up in her house. She braced herself for the door being kicked down. As she bent down to cover her naked body, someone knocked on the door.

"Who is it?" she yelled, already knowing the answer.

"Durham County police to serve you a restraining order."

"Restraining order?" she mumbled to herself. "Hold up. Let me throw something on, I'll be there in a minute," she told the officer.

She went upstairs and tossed on a pair of gym shorts and a

small, revealing tank top. She ran downstairs, still in her heels and out of breath. She unlatched the locks and pulled the door open.

""Here you go, ma'am," the officer presented her with the restraining order.

"Anthony B," the officer called out. "Can you get out of the way while he grabs his things?" The officer moved Neatra to the side to let Anthony B get inside the house.

"You called the police?" Neatra spat.

"Had to. Don't feel bad. I didn't." He went upstairs to their room. Neatra tried to follow him, but the cop held her back.

Ain't this about a bitch, Neatra thought.

Anthony B gathered his clothes. Money, jewelry, shoes, and everything except the things Neatra had bought for him: brought back to many bad memories. He made six trips in all. Then he left without so much as a goodbye.

CHAPTER 5

"He did what?" Tamra asked in disbelief.

"Hit me with a restraining order, like I'm some psychopath or something," Neatra told her.

Tamra held in her laughter, "Damn. He got you tripping out," That had to be some real good dick, she was telling herself.

"Hell yeah," Neatra admitted. "I haven't been able to sleep since he left."

"I told you all of your bullshit was going to catch up with you. All them men you cheated on him with. All the times you stole money out of his pants and stash. And what about that girl you jumped on for nothing?"

Neatra chuckled. "No. We. Because you know we jumped that bitch..."

Neatra was right. Tamra reminisced back to when they banked Kimbella. At first Kimbella was getting the best of her cousin Neatra. And then she jumped in. Couldn't have Kimbella thinking she could run through the family, Tamra smirked. She had to show Kimbella that she could get down in case she and

Anthony B were ever on the prowl together and that bitch wanted to try her gangster.

A voice snapped Tamra from her train of thought, "Say what?"

"I said Anthony B is worth fighting for."

"He definitely is," she kept it all the way hundred. Tamra had fought hard for him that night. Too bad you about to lose him when I put this magical pussy on him, Tamra said to herself.

***

Relationship specialist Mel Brooks glared at Tyler Anderson. "So what seems to be your problem?"

Tyler took a deep breath and unloaded his problems. "I don't know," he started. "I'm a good guy. I just don't know what's wrong with me. I just can't do anything good in her eyes."

"Who is she?"

"Nesha, counselor,"

"Just call me Doc,"

"Doc?" Tyler asked kind of skeptically.

"Like doctor Phil Good. Like you come to me with your problem, and I fix it," he told Tyler.

"Cool. So, about Nesha," he wanted to get back to the matter at hand.

"What about Nesha?" Doc asked.

"She is overly abusive."

"Like, what do you mean by overly abusive?" Doc questioned.

"She gets mad and just unleashes on me for no reason."

Tyler glanced down at the ground after his statement.

"Hold your head up. There is still hope for you after all," Doc stated. "So why does she beat on you for no reason?" he asked.

Tyler shrugged his shoulders, "I don't know. It's like I can't please her anymore," he openly admitted. "I can't remember that last time we..." he glanced around the room, "you know?"

"Had sex," Doc blurted out. This is interesting, he thought.

"Damn. You going to let everyone in Durham know."

"My bad. What goes on in here is only for my ears. Everything is confidential."

"And I'ma trying to keep it that way," Tyler responded. He was already embarrassed as it was to be seeking counseling. What if people at work found out? Better yet, what if Nesha found out? Then I'd be in deep shit. Just the thought of Nesha made him shut the hell up, like she could hear him talking shit about her. "Doc, can we set up a meeting some other time? I mean, I don't feel right talking about Nesha like this to someone else."

Doctor Mel took a deep huff of frustration. He really wanted to hear more of Tyler's problems. There was a saying: You never know how good your life was until you heard about how screwed up someone else's is. "Just remember, I'm only here to help you," he told Tyler, disappointed that he wouldn't get to hear more about Tyler's interesting story. He loved his job. He got paid just to listen to people vent about their love lives all day.

***

"You don't like me," specialist Mel Brooks stated to his

client Anthony Bryant.

"Damn. You're really good at this, counselor."

"Doc," Mel replied.

"Whatever," Anthony B remarked.

"It never amazes me when guys like you end up in here. Thinking that the whole world owes you something. The world doesn't owe you shit!" he shouted. "I know what to do with your tough ass." He picked up the phone.

Anthony B looked on, "What are you doing?"

"I'm calling the police and telling them they can come pick you up. It's no use at all trying to reach you. That's what's wrong with African American men," he muttered. "You act like you would rather be locked in that damn slammer than be in my session," he barked.

"Hold up," Anthony B protested. "Calm down. I never said I didn't want to be here. Put the phone down, bruh."

Doc held his laughter in. Chump, he thought. "I thought you would see things my way," he hung up the phone. He hated street thugs. They always felt that because they had drugs and guns, they ruled the world. "I'm not having you getting smart with me. I run shit in here. One more outburst — to the jail house you go. You can make this easy, or you can make it hard. Either way. I ain't going to jail."

"Cool, bruh. Just sit down. Anything you want, bruh," Anthony B stated.

Wasn't so tough! Now, Doc thought, "I know your kind," he said to Anthony B.

"And what's my kind?" Anthony B asked as he sat back in his chair and listened.

"The type that think just because they got a little money,

and street fame it makes them so much better than everyone else around them."

"I thought this was counseling," Anthony B remarked.

"It is. I'm about to give you some shit that will give you a different look on how you see life."

"I'm listening."

Doctor Mel didn't like smart mouths. And he sure as hell didn't like hustlers. He was about to do his best to make Anthony Bryant's life a living hell. "They said you would only have to take my class for a month. I'm going to request more time for you."

"But…" Anthony B started before he was rudely cut off.

"Don't but me. I can see right now that you think you in control. I'm requesting six months."

"You can't do that," Anthony B stood to his feet and overlooked Doc.

"What you going to do? Hit me. I'll sue. Get the fuck out of here before I call the cops on you."

"Asshole," Anthony B said under his breath.

"What you say, boy?" Mel held his finger to his own ear, "I can't hear you."

"Nothing, man."

"That's what I thought it was. Now raise the hell up out of my office and next time come in here with some damn sense, alright?"

Anthony B couldn't swallow his pride. "You not going to talk to me no any kind of way."

The doctor stepped from behind his desk, "Say what, do something." He stuck his chin out just enough for Anthony B to knock his ass off into whala-wonderland. "That's what I thought. You ain't going to do nothing. Get the fuck up out of here, bitch."

"What?" Anthony B had to restrain himself, "You know what? You right."

"I know. See you here tomorrow."

"I can't."

"Why not?"

"I have something to do."

Doc chuckled. "Looks like somebody likes jail."

"I'll be here. What time?" Anthony B hissed.

"Six in the morning."

"That's too early."

"Make it five in the morning."

"Come on, man," Anthony objected.

"Make it four a.m." Doc let his words linger.

Anthony B could sense where this argument was headed. He had no win here. Right about now he could wring Neatra's neck.

"I'll be here," he told Doc.

"Good. See you in 16 hours," Doctor Mel glanced at his watch. "It's almost lunch time. I'll walk you to your car."

"No, man, really. I'm cool."

"No, I insist," Doc walked Anthony B out of his office. "Let's take the elevator," he motioned. "You're going to like me," he said as they stepped into the elevator, "You can learn a thing or two from me. I'ma hell'va motherfucker," Doc stated.

Yeah, right, was the thought in Anthony B's head. When they reached the lobby, he tried going in his own direction.

"Come on, man. The parking lot is this way. Don't tell me you walked," Doc asked.

"No, actually I drove."

"Which one of these is your car?"

Before Anthony B could answer, his chauffeur pulled up with his Bentley.

"You ain't tell me you had a Bentley. Let's say we do lunch."

"Let's don't and say we did," Anthony B suggested. "See you in the a.m."

"Yeah. But before you leave," Doc looked inside of the spacious Bentley, Maybach as the chauffeur got out, "I think I'm going to have to charge you a little extra..."

"Do you?" Anthony B said as he got into the ride, and his chauffeur closed the door for him.

"I definitely will," Doc proclaimed as he looked on.

***

"Breathe. Take deep breaths. Relax your mind: Life is what you make it. What you bitches want from a nigga? How long will you mourn me? Thugs paradise. Dear momma, take it nice and slow, these are my confessions. When a woman's fed up," Doc sang in deep meditation.

Anthony B cocked one eye open. This asshole is crazy. First, he gets me up meditating at four in the morning. Then he has the nerve to be quoting famous rap and R&B slogans like they were his own phases.

"Lean back. Get jiggy wit it, I'm all the way up," Doc stated.

"What? This has to be the stupidest shit ever," Anthony B proclaimed.

"Relax. Don't interrupt my thoughts. Get behind me, Satan. You mean me no good," Doctor Mel spat.

Anthony B just minded his own business. He was so bothered by what Doc was doing that, he just stopped trying to meditate and watched him. I wonder how much it will cost me to have this fool killed, Anthony B was thinking silently.

"Can't nobody stop me, can't nobody hold me down, oh, no! I gotta keep on moving," Doc sang as he bobbed his head to the P. Diddy song.

Anthony B was fed up with all of the Doc's singing, "Are we finished with this session?"

"No. We still have things to do. Go over to my desk," he said to Anthony B. He continued to meditate as Anthony B did so, "Dear God, please let me help Anthony B. He's lost. But please help him become the man you want him to be. He may be a drug dealer, but Christ was just a sinner who fell down. We fall down, but we get up," he sang the gospel.

What are you? Some type of false prophet? Anthony was contemplating. He waited at the desk as Doc perpetrated the fraud.

When Doc got finished with his meditation, he walked over to his desk. He went into his desk drawer and pulled out a deck of cards.

"I'm not trying to play cards," Anthony B uttered.

"I'm just going to read your horoscopes."

"What the fuck are you doing?" Anthony B asked him.

"Close your eyes."

"You spooking me out."

"Nothing but tarot cards."

"I'm not doing this shit," Anthony B told Doc.

"Then don't. I will make sure the judge lays down the death penalty on you. You'll never hit a woman again as long as you live."

"I didn't hit her," Anthony B argued.

"Tell that to the judge." Doc put the cards down and picked up the phone instead. "You don't want me to do this," he threatened. "Clint Eastwood ain't got shit on me." He pressed the 9-1...

"Hold up. No," Anthony B gave in.

"Close your eyes and take a deep breath."

"For what?" Anthony B asked.

"So I can give you some valuable information."

"I thought you were a relationship counselor."

"I am. One of the best. Now close your eyes," Doc began to read the tarot cards. "I see death."

Anthony B asked with concern, "Who?"

"Someone close to you."

"Who?"

"Don't know."

"What else you see?"

"A Bentley."

"What else?"

"Prices going up on gas."

"What?"

"I see destruction. Headed-for-self-destruction."

"Self-destruction," Anthony B mocked.

"Yeah. I see a girl who's no good for you."

"What else do you see?"

"You hitting her. Stop it," he pleaded, "I see her begging you to stop."

Anthony B frowned, knowing Doc was on some bullshit. "What else do you see?"

"Trouble."

Anthony B played along, "What kind of trouble?"

"Handcuffs, jail time, domestic abuse charges, being away until you're old and gray. I see you begging rich people for food, shelter, bread," Doc claimed.

"Doesn't sound too good. What do I need to do?"

"Let me help you."

Anthony B burst out laughing, "You want me to follow you?"

"Yes, why not? I can help you."

"You're not fooling me. You're not a mind reader. And you sure as hell ain't no doctor. Is this even a real practice?" Anthony B chuckled.

"You got hate in your blood."

"Jadakiss, right?" Anthony B asked.

"Get out of my office!" Doctor Mel yelled out as he pointed to the door. "Don't come back!"

"Fuck you," Anthony B said to Doc.

"Homo," Doc shot back with his own assault.

"Fake."

"We'll see who's faking when I get done with you," Doc threatened.

"Do what you have to do. Ain't nobody scared of jail. Don't let me catch you out in these streets. Boom!" Anthony B blew his fingertip like it was a smoking gun.

"Get out," Doc screamed.

As if he needed to tell him, Anthony B slammed the door to the manipulating doctor's office. "Fake-ass relationship counselor," he mumbled as he left.

"Fake-ass American Gangster," Doc uttered. He debated whether to call the police, but chose not to. But what he would do was keep charging Anthony B for his services. Dumbass, he thought. A thousand bucks for each session for six months. Let's see. That's what. Three times a week for six months. 72,000, he added in his brain.

He needed to clear his head. He knew just the place. Doctor Mel Brooks told his secretary to reschedule all of his appointments for later on that afternoon. He then got into his drop-top Aston Martin and drove to the exotic strip club called Teasers. You had to have loot to go in Teasers. The people who frequented this club had money to blow. You know? Doctors, lawyers, businessmen, musicians, movie stars, athletes, etc.

He parked his car and got out. When I step up in the strip club. He paid his entry fee. All the ladies show some love. He was bumping that game track in his head when he saw the woman of his dreams. Lord, have mercy. He walked up to shawty, "Baby, you one of the coldest I done seen."

"You must be Tank," she smirked. "He's one of my favorite!" she said about the R&B singer.

"He ain't got shit on me. I'm relationship counselor Mel Brooks," he extended his hand out.

She took it. "Would you like a lap dance?"

"Two or three," he requested. "But not out here in public. I have to keep a low profile," he told her.

"I understand." Bingo, she thought. "Right this way," she said as she led Mel to the Red Light special.

CHAPTER 6

Anthony B answered his cell, "Speak."

"Someone told me they saw you in a brand-new Bentley," Neatra asked.

"Who told you that?"

"Who hasn't?" she responded. What made her much more upset was the fact that he hadn't let her ride in it. "When are you going to come and scoop me up and take me for a ride?"

"Can't," he said to her.

"Why not?" she wanted to know.

"Restraining order," he commented.

"That doesn't mean anything. I will not act crazy."

"And I ain't even going to give you the chance," Anthony B stated.

"Anthony B, I'm sorry. I made a mistake," she pouted.

"You did that," he hung up.

***

Neatra pretended like she wasn't hurt. But deep down inside

she was hurt. Fuck it. I'll fix him. She got up from the sofa and went to her bathroom, where she went into the closet and grabbed a bottle of Advil.

"We'll see how he feels when he finds out I'm dead," she assured herself as she swallowed the whole bottle of pills. After she did so she called Anthony B.

***

"What is it?" Anthony B barked into the phone.

"I feel sick," she slurred.

"What type of games you playing?"

"Games?" she frowned. "The rooms is spinning, I can't see. I'm dying."

"Neatra. Neatra!" he yelled. There was no reply. "Yo. Take me to the house," he told his chauffeur. "Step on it."

***

Anthony B made his way inside the house. "Neatra. Neatra. Where are you?" he called out. There was no reply.

The house was silent. Oh God. What if something happened to her? He wouldn't be able to live with himself. "Neatra!" he called out again. He checked the kitchen. Nothing. He checked the closets. Bedroom. He was running out of places to check.

He checked the bathroom in their room and saw Neatra slumped out on the floor. The last thing he needed was a body. He hoped like hell she wasn't dead. With the luck he was having, he knew he would be the primary suspect.

"Neatra. Hold on. Don't die on me," he said as he rushed to

her aid.

***

Anthony B paced the hospital floor at Duke Regional Hospital. He hoped like hell Neatra would pull it through. Things were getting crazy. As if the day couldn't have gone any worse, "Neatra's mom," he mumbled under his breath.

"What did you do to my daughter? You hit her again! You coward. Get'em, y'all!" She sicced her six nephews on Anthony B, all of which had been in and out of jail for racketeering charges, kidnapping, armed robberies, grand auto theft, jaywalking or purse snatching. These guys had done it or thought about it.

"Back the hell up," Anthony B drew his gun out. "Don't make me act ghetto," he warned all of them.

"Put the gun down, tough ass," Neatra's mom urged.

"So these fools can knock my head off? I want to see hands, and don't try nothing," he stated.

"Put down the gun and give me a one-on-one. I'll whip his ass," J-Doe commented.

"Bitch ass sucker," Kid'co stated.

"Your aunt," Anthony B retorted. Before he knew it, he was running through the hospital with six thirty-year-old gang bangers after him. He hit the staircase.

"We got that punk now," Kid'co pounded his hand into his palm. "I'm ready to die."

"You hit my cousin, fool," J-Doe punched the wall. "That's my first cousin," he cried out, tears forming around his heartless face.

"Let's rob this chump," Anthony B could hear them plotting

on him.

"You see that Bentley, Maybach outside? Fuck him! Let's go get that motherfucker," Lil Boo-boo commented.

"Lil Boo-boo, that you?" Anthony B asked as he looked up the staircase.

"This fool thinks he knows you," J-Doe spat.

"Yo. You still got that iPod I got you when you was in the joint (Jail)?" Anthony B asked.

"Man, fuck that iPod. Blood thicker than water. Let's wreck this fool," Boo-boo stated, giving chase with his cousins.

Anthony B reached the lobby. Neatra's cousins were on him. He knew he had one or two options: let off shots or meet an early death. He started licking off shots.

"Quit shooting in the air, punk," J-Doe stated as he gave chase.

"Boom," Anthony B shot and hopped into his ride. "Go," he told his driver.

***

J-Doe moaned, spun around, grabbed his kidney, flopped on the ground and started crying like a bitch, "I'm hit. He shot me."

***

What a night, Anthony B thought to himself, wondering whether he killed J-Doe. That fool asked for it. Talking that gangster shit. He tossed the gun he had shot J-Doe with out onto the highway. I need a drink. He reached for his cooler, pulled out a cold bottle of Remy Martin and started drinking.

"Where to?" the chauffeur asked.

"Just drive," he told his driver." I probably killed that asshole. He thought about J-Doe. What if this fool died, or worse? What if he pressed charges? And what about that bitch ass counselor/mind reader/scam artist/sissy boy that called himself Doc? What if he contacted the authorities? Or even worse. What if Neatra didn't pull through? He could see her mom taking the witness stand on him. And her six minus one nephews, if J-Doe didn't pull through, just mashing their fists in their hands and popping their knuckles at him. He was sure that he would bump into one or two of them on state if he got jailed. Damn. What a night. He needed answers. Shit was crazy!

What the... He jumped up as his cell rang. He grabbed his heart and thought, I almost jumped out of my skin, laughing about his paranoia as he took the call.

"Hello."

"Hello, who is this?"

"Tamra."

"Oh. What up." Like he didn't already know. He hoped for the best and braced himself for the worst, "Is Neatra okay?"

"Yeah. They just pumped her stomach."

"Pumped her stomach?" he repeated. "For what?"

"She overdosed, but she's better now," Tamra brought to his attention.

"Damn," he uttered out.

"She can leave the hospital tomorrow. I will take her home."

"Word. Good looking out," Anthony stated.

"It's nothing," Tamra assured.

"Oh yeah, I almost forgot, what happened to J-Doe?"

"You mean, like, if he pressed any charges or not?" Tamra asked.

"Exactly."

"Well," she paused. "The good news is he didn't press charges. His pride wouldn't allow him. The bad news is he said it isn't over. You better watch out for them numbskulls."

He laughed.

"You know I'm right," she stated seriously.

"Yeah. Good looking out. Can I speak to Neatra?"

"Nope. I don't think that's a good idea. I had to sneak downstairs just to let you know what was going on. But if you want to talk to Neatra, then just call my phone about 3 p.m. tomorrow, and she'll be at my house."

"Cool. Make sure you keep an eye on her for me."

Tamra giggled. "I will," she said before ending the call.

The next day Neatra's mom waited for her daughter to wake up. "You have to be one messed up heffa. I know that child's dick isn't that damn good that it has you trying to kill your damn self."

Neatra's vision was blurry from her current overdose. "I'm not trying to hear that. Where is Anthony B?" were the first words to come out of her mouth.

"Well, I'll be damned. Seems like you should be more concerned about what happened to your cousin J-Doe." Neatra's mom spat.

"What happened to J-Doe?" Neatra sympathized.

"Anthony B shot him. That's what happened to him," her mother explained. "And all because we thought he put his hands on you."

"Anthony B wouldn't do that..." Neatra said, but her mother cut her off.

"Why you keep protecting this fool? You don't need him. I'm

taking you up out of this hospital, and you're bringing your ass home with me," Neatra's mom declared.

This bitch got it all planned out, Neatra said in the back of her mind. "I'm not leaving my baby mansion to stay with you and them got-damn roaches," Neatra acknowledged. "Can't stand them crawling on me."

"You grew up with roaches in the house. So what happened from now until then?" Neatra's mom asked.

"Anthony B," Neatra answered. It was as if God knew she wasn't trying to go back to her mother's house with those roaches and rats, just as if God heard her call: Tamra walked into the room.

"You ready to go?" Tamra questioned Neatra.

"Been ready. Thanks, Mom. But I have to go get my man," Neatra sprang up out of bed. "You's got to be the craziest heffa in this world. Ain't no dick on the planet that good," Neatra's mom proclaimed.

"That is where you're wrong. And I would rather be getting some of it instead of being cramped up in this hospital with your lonely ass," Neatra explained.

"May be lonely, but tell you one thing: I'm not a damn fool."

"My father didn't think so," Neatra retorted.

"Ain't nothing gon' come good to you but ass whippings," Neatra's mom told her.

"Until then I'ma be with with my man," Neatra snapped her fingers in acknowledgement.

"Come on, girl," she said to Tamra.

"If you need me, you know how to get in touch with me," she kissed her mom on the cheek. "I'm sorry about all I said. But Anthony B is a good man. Remember when he paid your rent a year straight when you were sick and out of work?"

"I thought that was you," Neatra's mom questioned.

"Nope. You know I look too good to work," Neatra flipped her long gorgeous weave up in the air, being boujee. "I haven't worked since I left your place. And that was..." she did the math in her head, estimating, "almost nine years."

"Nine years is a long time to be shacking up without marriage," Neatra's mom said to her.

"Who said I want marriage? I just want what I want when I want. Anthony B is the best that happened to me since welfare cheese and food stamps."

"I know, that's right," Tamra thought out loud. Anthony B was a hoe's savior. It's not that she despised her cousin. She just despised the way she treated such a good man. Now if the shoe was on the other foot, Anthony B would be good because he would've had her and not Neatra's treacherous ass. "Let's get out of here," she said to Neatra.

"Where are we headed?" Neatra asked.

"You're going to be staying with me for a couple of days," Tamra gave confirmation. "I don't want to stay with you. I want to go home with my Boo," Neatra stopped and frowned.

"You better come on with me before I let you go home with your mother," Tamra said between clenched teeth.

Neatra thought about the roaches and rats and said, "Come on. I'm going with you." It was a no-brainer.

CHAPTER 7

Doc listened as Tyler addressed some of his issues about his abusive girlfriend Nesha. "Your situation is unlike any I've come across," he stroked his goatee. "I think you should see if Nesha wants to come with you to some of our sessions."

"Are you crazy? Do you know what she'd do if she knew I was talking to you?" Tyler told Doc.

"Right," Doc remarked, still stroking his goatee. You could see he was in deep thought. "I think I have a plan for you."

"What is it?"

"Give her the silent treatment. Let her go and come as she pleases. Never once asking where she's been or where she's going. Just meditate, and don't forget: breath in, breath out. Now help me say it."

"Breath in, breath out," Tyler chanted.

"Good. I think you're ready now. Be strong and of good courage."

"The Bible?" Tyler questioned.

"Yeah. Always remember: If God is for you, who can be

against you?" Doc answered. Tyler nodded his head in agreement. Doc was a really inspirational speaker, and one of the best people he had ever come into the presence of.

***

Tyler was finding out that Doc's sessions were actually doing him some good. He had been meditating day and night. And it seemed that his main focus wasn't on Nesha. He had been paying her less and less attention. No more worrying, no more giving a damn whether she stayed out all night, no more asking where she was going, or when she was coming back. Just like Doc suggested. He smiled as he walked into Doctor Mel's office.

"Hello, Doc."

"Hello, Tyler. How have things been going?"

"Just fine. Well, actually, beautiful," Tyler stated.

"Someone must've gotten a little love and affection?" Doc nudged Tyler with his arm.

"No."

Doc stroked his goatee, "Has she been talking to you?"

Tyler thought about the question that was raised. "No."

"You mean to tell me that she hasn't said two words to you this whole week?"

"And vice versa," Tyler acknowledged.

"Oh God," Doc walked around in a circle, like he was trying to figure things out.

Tyler was getting worried as Doc burned up the carpet with his pacing around. "Is something wrong?"

"Yes. Very much. Why haven't you talked to her?" Doc

questioned.

"Because you told me not too."

"Right. But now I'm having a change of heart." Doc stopped pacing back and forth.

"What are you saying?" Tyler wanted to know.

"That you may need to swallow your pride and correspond with the woman you love, you fool."

"What?" Tyler glared at Doc with a strange expression.

"What are you looking at me for? You need to be out there, trying to save your relationship."

"But…" Tyler was about to say something when Doc cut him off.

"Go," Doc pointed toward the door. " Go save your relationship."

"How?" Tyler asked as he rose to his feet.

"Teddy P. Turn down the lights," he gestured toward the door.

"Thanks, Doc. You're the best!"

Doc sat on his desk as Tyler left. The truth was, he was having what writers call writer's block, athletes call slump and what a scared singer calls stage fright. Guess what, you could call his situation: a midlife crisis.

He was voted Essence's best relationship counselor. Truth be told, he couldn't even help his own relationships. He felt kind of bad about not being able to help Tyler in his difficult situation. And what about Anthony B? Anthony B was the only one who had figured out that he was nothing but a con artist stealing money as it came his way.

Fuck Anthony B, Doc thought. He sure could use a drink. A blunt. A girl with nice tits and ass. He left his office. Told his secretary to reschedule all of his afternoon appointments for a later date. Then he went to his favorite strip club.

***

Nesha walked into the house with Tyler Jr. in his car seat. What the hell is this? She glanced around. Damn. This man has gone all out, she was thinking. Rose petals were leading toward the bedroom. Candles were lit. An suddenly a sharp pain hit her in the heart. She had been entertaining D'angelo. I hope he doesn't want sex. I might just have to suck his dick. D'angelo got my pussy sore already. The last thing I need is for Tyler to ask me for some sex right now.

She carried Tyler Jr. up the stairs. She could hear Teddy P singing "Turn Off the Lights" on the radio in their bedroom.

"Oh shit!" she mumbled under her breath. This man is going to want some coochie. Her assumption was right. Tyler was lying on the bed, just as solid as a rock. The print in his briefs told that he hadn't had sex in a very long time.

She could've kicked herself for giving her love to D'angelo. She didn't know what she saw in that man, but his great ability to please her between the sheets. And even though she had a good man at home, she continued fucking with D'angelo just for a great fuck.

"What's all this?" she asked with her eyes wide open.

Tyler got out of bed. "Well, you know," he grabbed his son along with the car seat, "thought I would do a little something nice for you since we haven't been on good terms lately."

Nesha replied, "Oh."

"Well, put Tyler Jr. in his baby crib while I go freshen up."

Lord, was she in deep shit. D'angelo's scent was all over her.

"Word. But, before you go, let me get a kiss."

Nesha swallowed the lump that formed in her throat. "Hold on until I go freshen up. My love for you isn't going anywhere, big daddy," she said back to him as she looked at his enormous erection. Gosh, she thought to herself. Two big dicks in one night. She hurried to the bathroom, ran hot water in the tub. She had to tighten up her kitty cat, so she used the old vinegar trick. Her pussy was like new. She sprinkled on scents of peaches over her entire body, head to toe. What was she going to do now? She hoped like hell Tyler would be satisfied with just a little oral sex. Damn. She had forgotten to grab her undergarments.

She opened the bathroom door and tried to tiptoe across the room unnoticed. "Damn, Nesha, what are you about to do?" Tyler asked.

"About to put on my red thong and matching bra. You know, your favorite." She covered her body as much as she could with her two hands.

"Nah. I like it better with the clothes off. Let me see that body," he examined his future wife. "You look magnificent. I always thought you were the best-looking bitch alive."

Normally she would've been offended. But to tell the truth, she was flattered. She blushed. "Thanks," she said in response.

"What's wrong with you tonight? Why you acting so shy?" He stood up, walked over to her and covered his arms around her like a blanket.

He kissed the nape of her neck. "I know it's been a long time, but daddy is going to rock that shit tonight," he whispered into her ear.

Oh Gosh! Nesha could feel his swell rising against the back of her thigh. She had to do something. She pushed him back onto the bed and gave head like she had never given it before.

She wrapped her mouth around him like vise-grip pliers. She bobbed up and down until she could see him grabbing shit. The pillow, the bed sheets. She had him grabbing her head and all. Normally she didn't play that shit. But tonight, she was too exhausted from her rendezvous with D'angelo. She just wanted to get Tyler to get his nut and take his horny ass to sleep.

Her jaws were sore from sucking two dicks in one night. And on top of that Tyler wouldn't climax for shit. She wanted to kick him. What the fuck was he on? Ecstasy or Viagra. She must've sucked him for an hour straight, and he still hadn't busted off.

Tyler scanned through Nesha's hair with his hand. Tonight, he was holding himself for just the right time. He needed to save his relationship. "Get up," he told her.

"What?" she managed to say with a pipe engulfed halfway down her throat. She looked at him like he had gone crazy, "What? Am I not satisfying you?" she asked with stretched-open eyes.

"Believe me, I'm satisfied," he pulled her up from all fours. "I want some of that bomb ass pussy."

"I'm not done giving you a blow job," she tired kneeling into a squatting position.

"Who cares. I want some of that pussy," he lifted her back up. "Turn that ass around," he smacked her on her rear end.

"Okay," she swallowed the lump in her throat. "Don't be too rough."

He knew when she said that she meant the exact opposite.

He turned her around and entered her from the rear, "Damn, this pussy dry as fuck! Hold on," He kneeled down and started eating her coochie.

She protested, "No, Tyler!"

"Yes," he stuck his tongue inside her.

She turned around and pushed his head away. She had a guilty conscience about sleeping with D'angelo earlier. She couldn't let him stoop that low. Was this God's way of making her see the light? By letting her know that she couldn't have her cake and eat it too?

Tyler thought he was pleasing her, but he was actually making her feel like someone had poured salt in her womb. "Ahh," she yelped.

"Feel good, doesn't it?" he asked.

Hell no, she told herself. "Fuck all the foreplay." Her legs were burning like she had burns on her coochie. "Let's get this over with," she complained. "Let me have it."

"I love it when you talk dirty to me," Tyler entered Nesha from the back.

A sharp pain ripped through Nesha. Got damn. Tyler was stout for a white man.

"I've been waiting a long time for this. It's been almost three or four months and four days. I'm about

to tear this pussy up." Whop-whop-whop, was the only sound that could be heard.

"Oh God," Nesha cried out in excruciating pain. "You're hurting me."

"Damn this pussy is tight, girl. I'm about to go long." He took a deep thrust with his pelvis and said, "Hard." He dug a little deeper as he gripped her waist and pulled her down onto his erection. "Feel that?" he held her as still as possible to let her marinate on his erection.

"Yes," she cussed and fussed.

"Tell me who this pussy belongs too?"

"You," she screamed out.

"Whose?" he asked again to make sure.

"Yours," she shouted.

"Spell it out."

"T.Y.L.E.R."

"That's my name," Tyler fucked Nesha good and hard, careful not to come too fast. He knew he had to go hard to save his relationship. And that's exactly what he did. He fucked Nesha for well over an hour and a half.

Nesha lay beside Tyler and contemplated. She rubbed his cute face as he slept like a baby. "I love you," she mouthed to herself. What the fuck had she been thinking? How could she have the best man in the world and lose him for a slug with no job, staying with his motherfucking mom and shit, and not even that good-looking? D'angelo was OK as far as looks go; resembled Buster Rhymes. But Tyler was all that and then some more. The closest comparison to him was the soccer player David Beckham. So why couldn't she stop fucking with D'angelo's bum ass?

***

Tyler chilled in Doc's office with his feet kicked up on the table and his hands behind the nape of his neck. "Shit couldn't be better. Not only am I getting sex three to four times a day, but I'm eating steak and caviars, shrimp, lobster, and oysters and shit," Tyler told Doc. "You ever sip champagne and get head at the same time?" he questioned.

"That's some gangster shit," Doc replied.

"Yeah. Well, I'm gangster," Tyler popped his collar. "I'm afraid I won't be needing your classes anymore."

The doctor took a deep sigh, "There's nothing more I can do for you," he admitted. Things were looking good for Tyler. "I'm going to hate to see you leave."

"And I'm going to hate to leave," Tyler rose from his chair and extended his hand. "Thanks, Doc."

"The pleasure was all mine," he hugged Tyler.

Tyler patted Doc on the back, "Yo. I know you aren't crying."

"Nah, man," Doc lied, "I'm too gangster for that."

"Stay that way. Catch you later," Tyler said to Doc.

Doc stared at Tyler like a proud parent.

CHAPTER 8

"What the fuck is going on?" Neatra screamed. "Somebody trying to kill us?" she hollered out. "Call the police!"

"Shut up," Tamra told her. "My lights just went out. Let me find my purse so I can locate a lighter. Get off of me," Tamra nudged Neatra in her side as she stepped onto her heels.

"I'm scared," Neatra told Tamra. "This shit ain't cool. Why didn't you pay your bills?"

"Why do you think? I got fired from my job," Tamra stated the obvious.

"Oh, why didn't you tell me?"

"You have enough shit going on," Tamra commented. Like trying to kill your damn self, she was thinking while she searched for her purse.

"But you knew I would've lent you some money. You're my cousin."

"Not right now, Neatra," Tamra spat. "I don't feel like hearing that shit."

"Well, you need to hear it. I'm not staying here with no lights," Neatra frowned. Tamra lit up a few candles. "Then what are we going to do?"

"Let's go to my place," Neatra suggested. She couldn't wait to be in the comfort of her own home. She had no complaints about staying with Tamra. But quiet as it's kept, she wanted to see her Boo.

Tamra drove to Neatra's house. She was really concerned about how Neatra would react if Anthony B didn't take her back. She couldn't say that she would blame him if he didn't. After all, Neatra was a far cry from wifely material.

Tamra pulled her 2008 Camry behind Nesha's Benz.

"Anthony B is here. Both of his rides are in the driveway," Neatra said as she got out of the car.

Tamra only hoped Neatra didn't play herself. She had jumped up out of the car and had sprinted to the house before Tamra could even lock the car doors.

"Anthony B," Neatra shouted. She rushed to him, wrapped her arms around him and gave him a passionate hug. "I miss you," she told him.

"Yo, you know you aren't supposed to be within 500 feet from me," he said to her.

Tamra smirked.

Neatra explained, "Tamra lights got cut off. We had no lights. We couldn't see." Tamra frowned. Neatra only added to her embarrassment.

"We had to use candles. I was scared," she continued to hug Anthony B. "Me and Tamra are going to stay here," she told him.

"Cool. I will leave."

She felt a sharp pain in her heart. "Don't go," she begged, "I need you. I love you. I can't be without you."

Tamra wanted to say, "Get a grip, Neatra." But it was too late. Neatra was on Anthony B's brand-new Jordan's.

"See. This the shit I'm talking about right here," he looked down at Neatra.

"Please don't go. I need you," she cried.

Anthony B looked at Tamra. " Yo. Get your cousin."

"Neatra," Tamra tried helping Neatra up.

"Get off me," she fought Tamra off. "I love you, Anthony B," she cried out. "I'm sorry. I messed up. Just stay home. I need you. I need you," her chest heaved. "I'll do anything. Just tell me what I have to do."

"Don't do this shit," he freed himself up. "Tamra, take her upstairs," he requested.

"Anthony B," Neatra whined.

"Go. And don't come the fuck out of that room until I tell you. Don't make me call the police on your crazy ass," he warned. "Go."

"But…" she half-said.

"Go," he pointed to the staircase.

"Come on, Neatra," Tamra wrapped her arms around her cousin.

"What if I get hungry?" Neatra asked.

He hissed. "Get Tamra to fix you something to eat."

Neatra's gaze hit the floor in defeat. "I love you," she said before Tamra helped her up the steps and to the bedroom.

That girl is crazy. Anthony B shook his head in annoyance. He sat down on his leather sofa, grabbed the remote to the CD player and turned on his Rick Ross album. He lit a blunt and tried to get a level head. He knew Neatra was half-crazy, but the truth of the matter was that he still loved her.

He was listening to that "Maybach Music" as Tamra walked down the steps.

"Yo, Tamra," he called out.

"Yes, Anthony B."

"What are you about to do? Can you cook me something to eat?" he wanted to know.

"Got you," she replied.

"Word. It's been a long time since a brother had a decent meal around here."

Tamra knew that was the truth. Neatra couldn't cook a lick. "What do you have a taste for?"

"Cube steak, fried rice, carrots, green beans, and cornbread. You think you can handle that?"

"I can handle anything," she said in response.

She went into the kitchen and started preparing the meal. She had been in the kitchen for ten or twenty minutes when Anthony B walked in. "Something smells good," he took a sniff.

She laughed, "How come every time I come over here you ask me to cook?"

"Because you can. Plus, your cousin keeps a brother eating like a bum. Not the boss that he is."

Whose fault is that? she wondered. "When was the last time since you had a home cooked meal?"

"Since the last time you cooked it," he remarked.

"Since last Christmas?"

"Yep."

"That's crazy," she stated.

"Tell me about it," he passed the blunt to her.

"You're playing my jam," she started dancing to the beat and singing along.

"Would have come back for you, I just needed time to do what I had to do. Caught up in the life, I can't let it go. Whether that's right, I will never know, but here goes nothing," Drake chanted.

Tamra passed the blunt back to him, and he hit a few times and passed it back to her. His dick was getting harder by the second as he watched Tamra groove and cook at the same time. She was multitasking, he thought as he hit the blunt a few times and passed it back to her.

Tamra was chinky eyed from the exotic weed Anthony B had. She grabbed the blunt he passed to her and took a puff. "You got the blunt all wet. Nasty," she informed him.

They both laughed. They talked and kicked it until Tamra got through cooking. She fixed Anthony B a plate. "Here you go. I'm about to go upstairs with Neatra." She juggled two plates in her hand to take upstairs.

"Hold up," he called out to Tamra.

"What is it?" she stopped.

"Thanks for watching out for Neatra for me."

"No problem."

"I appreciate that," he said to her.

She smiled before she went upstairs.

***

Anthony B got dressed. As he was about to leave the house, he made a quick detour to the guest room Tamra was sleeping in. He eased the door open to let himself in. He walked over to the bed where Tamra slept peacefully. Her breasts were partly hanging out of her tank top, exposing her teat. He tapped her awake.

"Anthony B. What are you doing in here?" she asked.

"Last time I checked, I paid the bills, and this was my house,"

"What is it?" she covered herself.

"Wasn't nobody looking at you," he lied and half-chuckled.

"There ain't nothing funny. What are you doing in here?" she wanted to know.

"How come you ain't tell me you was having problems paying your light bill?" he questioned.

"Because. I'll get them cut back on," she told him. "I lost my job, so things been kind of rough. I'll get them back on," she replied.

"Facts," he tossed her a stack of money.

"I can't take this from you."

"Then pay me back. Either way, I don't give a shit! You are family," was his look on things. "No, Anthony B," she got out of bed. "Here," she placed the money back into his hands, "I can't take this."

Anthony B glanced down at the gap between Tamra's legs. "Damn, girl. I know we family and all. But you better put on some clothes before it be on like a pile of neck bones," he didn't try to hide his gaze.

"Oh shit," she commented. It dawned on her that she had on some skimpy as boy shorts. "I'm so sorry," she rushed to toss on her jeans.

"Damn, girl. I'm family," he teased.

"Shut up," she slid into her pants. "Thank you. But I wouldn't feel right taking your money."

"And I wouldn't feel right having you with your lights out.

Here, girl," he took the money she had given back to him and tossed it back to her in the knot it was in. "Stop being so independent," he told her. "Swallow your pride," he said, as he rubbed the side of her face with his thumb.

She was about to say something when he cut her off.

"Don't say shit. And don't tell Neatra," he stated before he left.

Tamra took a deep sigh as she sat across the bed. Damn. This is a whole lot of money, she thought as she started counting. And what the tally came up to was 5,000. I'm about to get my lights turned back on and do some shopping, she squealed.

***

Tamra had taken on a new job just so she could pay her bills. The work wasn't hard. But she sure hated what she was doing.

"Excuse me, can I get a dance?" asked a guy in a very expensive suit who kind of looked like the actor Tyler Perry.

"Yes, right this way," she led him to the V.I.P. room where she performed a sexy routine for him. This was no ordinary man. He had money to blow. She could tell by the money he was sprinkling on her.

"What's your name?" he inquired.

"Tamra," she spun around to face him. "Do you want another dance?"

"Yes. How much to buy the V.I.P.?" he smiled.

"The V.I.P.?" she commented. "I don't even know if you can do that."

"Then go find out. I don't want nobody in here but you and me. I don't want all these motherfuckers in my business," he glanced around.

"Okay. Be back in a minute," Tamra went to get her boss and told him what the gentleman had requested.

Tamra went back over to the gentleman and informed him, "He said for a thousand bucks you can have it."

"That's all?" He went into his pocket and counted out a stack. Then he counted out another stack, "That's for you, Momma. Hurry back."

Tamra shook her ass all night. And at the end of the night she gave the big-time spender her cell number. He had spent well over 3,000 on her. Not bad for her first night, Tamra thought. Things could only get better. She had things down to a science. She would steal the big-time paying customer from the club and make him her sugar daddy!

CHAPTER 9

"Nesha waited for Tyler to come home from work. Real talk. He had her gone off the pipe. Like for real. She was treating him like King Imhotep. As soon as she heard a crack of the door, she grabbed up Tyler's plate and took it to him, "Hey, honey!" She gave him a kiss. "How was your day?"

"Same ole shit," he huffed. "I'm exhausted."

"Here is your food. Let me go grab you a Heineken from the refrigerator."

He pulled her back to him, "Yo. You have to get a job or something and start helping out with some of these bills."

She swallowed the lump in her throat, "I ain't working."

"I'm serious," he told her.

"I'm serious, too."

"Fuck it," he let her go, "I'm gone."

"Where are you going?" she commented.

"Don't ask me where I'm going. Just pack me a lunch," he declared.

Nesha swallowed the lump in her throat, "Be right back. Let me wrap this in some aluminum foil," she said.

"Hurry up," he shouted.

Nesha rushed to the kitchen, wrapped Tyler's food up and then hurried back to him with his food in hand.

"It's still hot. Where are you going? When are you coming back?" she questioned.

"Don't ask no questions. Give me my damn food, woman," Tyler stated and left.

Nesha held a hand on her rising chest. What had gotten into Tyler? she asked herself. Her mind wondered. On top of that, Tyler Jr. had woken up and started crying. "Not right now," she uttered. She had other things on her mind right now to be worrying about some crying ass baby, "Shut up," she hollered as she picked up the phone and dialed up Tyler's number.

"Hello," he answered.

"When are you coming home?" she wanted to know.

"When I get back. Hey, I know that isn't my son crying like that?" he snapped.

She had been so worried about Tyler's whereabouts that she had totally forgotten about her son crying upstairs at the top of his lungs.

She ran upstairs with the cordless phone to her ear. "Shush, baby. Momma's here. You want to speak to your dad-dad?" she placed the phone to his ear as she sat and bounced him on her lap to stop him from crying.

When he stopped he-heing and gi-gaing, she put the phone up to her ear, "You still there?"

"You got to be the dumbest woman in the world," he told her. "I know you heard my fucking son crying if I heard him, and I'm not even at home. What the fuck is wrong with you?" he said out of frustration.

"I'm sorry. I'm here with him now, so I don't see the big deal," she couldn't even finish her statement before she heard the dial tone. Not being the one to be played by a lame ass man, she dialed his number right back. "You better talk to me and let me know what's going on." She couldn't believe it: She had been sent directly to voicemail.

That stupid-ass-son-of-a-bitch. I'ma kill'em, she promised, tossing her cell on the bed and pacing around the room with Tyler Jr. in her arms. She was worried. Tyler had never walked out on her and their son.

She called Tyler's mother, "Hello, Ms. Anderson. Have you seen Tyler? He left and never came back."

"Good," Ms. Anderson responded. "He should've left you a long time ago," she hung up.

I hate that bitch. She called his best friend, Key. "Key, have you seen or heard from Tyler? He hasn't been back home, and I am worried about him."

Key laughed, "I see somebody is finally standing up to the wicked witch of the west?" he laughed.

"Clown," she said before hanging up.

Damn. Where is this idiot? She started thinking like a man. Strip club. Library. No. Too late. It's almost twelve in the morning. A bitch house. A bitch named. One person came to mind. She wrapped Tyler Jr. in a blanket and tossed him into his car seat. Then she was off, like a bitch trying to locate her man.

She drove to Amber's house. For some reason she just didn't trust her best friend. She pulled in front of Amber's house and hopped out with the car lights still on. She banged on Amber's door, the whole time checking to see whether Tyler's car was nearby.

Amber opened the door, yawning in her robe. She was surprised to see Nesha standing at the door. "What are you doing here?"

Nesha stood on her tiptoes and peered behind Amber to see whether her man was in the house. "Nothing," she replied.

"I know that isn't Tyler Jr. out in the car," Amber double-checked. "Are you coming in?"

"No. I have to go," Nesha remarked.

That's weird, Amber thought as Nesha walked off and hopped into the car.

Nesha drove all around Durham, NC twice, looking for Tyler. She even drove by Amber's a few times: three, or four, five, maybe six times. If you asked her, Amber was a part-time hater. Just jealous because she didn't have a great man like Tyler, a man who looked good, fucked great, and would bring her the moon and stars — like Tyler would do for Nesha.

She got tired and drove back to the house. She could see Tyler's car in their parking lot and got happy. "Dad-dad's home," she said as Tyler Jr. was sleeping peacefully in the backseat of the car.

She parked, unlocked the car doors, got Tyler Jr. and went to the house. She closed the door behind her. She was startled by Tyler's presence. Her chest heaved. "You scared me."

"Where in the fuck you been with my son?" Tyler asked in the dark, sipping his favorite brew, Heineken. "Got my son out here in the middle of the night doing no telling what," he took a gulp of his brew.

"I was looking for you. You left without telling me where you were going. I've been calling your phone."

"You called everyone's phone, Nesha," he raised his voice. He started naming people, "My Mom, Key..."

"Key. Fuck him. He ain't nothing but a hater," she declared.

"You're really getting out of pocket. I don't know what else to do," he informed her.

"What do you mean?" she asked in a confused state of mind.

Tyler rubbed his head, "I love you. I really do. But I can't just do this anymore." He got up from the chair.

"Tyler, what are you talking about?" Nesha remarked. She was in a state of shock. "Don't leave us. You can't leave. Key doesn't know shit. I don't know what kind of shit he has put inside of your head," she stood in front of him with Tyler Jr. in her arm, and the other arm against the door.

"Please don't leave. I'll do anything," she sobbed, "I'll get a job like you asked. Just don't leave me. Just don't leave us. Let's get married," she pleaded with him.

"Move. Get your crazy ass out in front of this door, bitch. It's over," he stated.

"Bitch?" She snapped out, "Your momma the bitch, and you the bitch that came out of her." She took a swing at Tyler and missed, almost dropped her son on the ground, but Tyler thought fast and caught him, right before she knocked some sense into his ass. "Get your bitch ass upstairs and close the door," she placed her finger to his temple and gave it a shove.

"Nah, bitch. I'm tired of your shit," he pushed Nesha into the wall with one hand and sat Tyler Jr. onto the floor with the other. He pressed his hand around Nesha's neck. "The next time you put your hands on me, I'ma kill your stanking ass, bitch." He let her neck go as she slithered to the floor and hit the ground, making a thrusting sound. He could no longer stand her.

All the love and passion he had once had for her was gone. He raised his hand. "Don't hit me," Nesha yelled out.

"Never. I love you. I really do. I just think we need some time apart," and with that he left.

"Tyler," Nesha called out, "Tyler," she cried, "Don't leave me, don't leave!"

She got up off the floor. She knew she had to hurry if she wanted to stop Tyler from leaving. "Tyler," she called out, only to see him pulling off. "No, Lord." Her worst fear. Tyler had left her.

***

Nesha was in church with Tyler Jr. first thing that Sunday morning, praying to get her man back.

"Lord, I'm sorry," she prayed, "I promise not to cheat or treat Tyler bad again. I promise to stop messing with D'angelo's no good ass. I promise to straighten up and fly right. I promise to find a job and help him out with the bills. Lord, I promise to dwell in the house of the Lord, forever! Just please! Bring Tyler back."

Almost as if God was trying to speak to her, the church choir started singing. "Can't sleep at night. And you wonder why. Cause maybe God is trying to tell you something."

Nesha began to cry, "Yes, Lord," she screamed out.

"Do I hear somebody asking the Lord into their lives today?" the pastor of the congregation asked.

"Yes, Lord," Nesha screamed out, "I need him in my life."

"Then come up to the aisle. We fall down but we get up," the pastor stated as the choir started singing Donnie McClurkin's song.

***

After she left the church, she called Tyler's phone. "Please let him answer. Lord, please!" she begged as she held the phone to her ear, driving at the same time.

"Hello."

"Tyler, guess what," Nesha excitedly asked.

He replied, "What?"

"I just took our son to church. And guess what else. I got saved."

"Good for you," Tyler uttered.

"What?" she couldn't believe him, out of all people, wasn't as happy as she was.

"This is supposed to be my moment right now. How come you're not happy for me? I'm a changed woman now," she informed him about the great news.

"Shit just doesn't change overnight. Everything has a process," he declared.

"Tyler, I'm trying. I really am. I will do anything. And I do mean anything to have you back in my life. I promise. Just come back home. I'll show you that I can be the woman you want me to be."

"I wish it was that easy. Sometimes you have to lose something to realize what you had," he told her.

"I know I messed up, but I'll show you that I'll do whatever it takes to win you back. Just come back home," she practically begged.

Tyler took a deep sigh, "Nesha, I'm happy that you got saved and all. But it's going to take more than that."

"What's it going to take?" she asked as she pulled up to their apartment and put the car in park.

"A lot of work," he told her.

"Does that mean you're coming back home?" she smiled at his reply.

"No, it means I'm going to be at my mother's house."

Nesha took a hard swallow, "Tyler, don't give up on us."

"I'm not sure you're the person I fell in love with. I mean, you used to be so sweet, so loving, so about me. Now it's all about what makes you happy," he said to her..

"You make me happy," she claimed.

"I can't tell."

"Tell me we wasn't having the best sex in the world. So what happened to make you leave?" she questioned.

"Something wasn't right," he said.

"What do you mean something wasn't right?" she shot back.

"Just don't think that I'm some kind of idiot. That's all," he emphasized.

"What are you talking about?"

"See, that's the shit right there," he smirked in annoyance. "Always playing me for a sucker."

"I don't know what I did," she placed her head on the steering wheel.

"I will tell you this: You really fucked up."

"How?" she managed to ask. She found herself starting to cry.

"Look. I really don't feel like talking right now," he let her know.

"Then when will you feel like talking to me?" she questioned.

"I don't know."

"That's all?" she asked.

"What else is there to say?"

"I'm not losing you. I will fight good and hard until you realize that you mean everything to me. You're the air that I breath. You're a big part of me," she started doing poetry.

"Miss me with that poetry," he cut her off.

"But… but…"

"But shit. Call me only about my son. Cause that's all it's really about."

"You don't mean that," she told him.

"Bye, woman."

"No, no," she pleaded.

"I have to go. I don't have time for this," he ended the connection.

Nesha cried. She looked over in the passenger seat, and Tyler Jr. was also crying, as if he also knew that she had fucked up.

***

"Back again, I see," Doc said to Tyler. "The last time I checked, you were doing so good."

"I know. It's just…" Tyler held his head down low.

"Hold your head up, young man," Doc patted Tyler on the back. "Tell me the problem," he smoothed Tyler's back.

Tyler glared at Doc's hand. "No homo."

"My bad," Doc removed his hand. "No homo either. Your problem?"

Tyler was starting to wonder whether Doc was gay. He shook off his thoughtful accusations, "Someone told me that Nesha was at the hotel with some guy."

"Who? What guy?" This shit is interesting.

"I don't know. But if I catch this fool..." Tyler stated.

Doc rubbed his chin hair in deep thought, "I knew she was no good."

"Ain't no good," Tyler repeated what Doc had confirmed.

Doc inquired, "Do you still see her?"

"No," he frowned, getting annoyed at Doc.

"What about your son? Do you go pick him up?"

"No."

"You better. She might have you paying child support if you don't. This woman is grimy." Doc got to the cold truth, "She can't be trusted."

Tyler took a deep breath. He knew Doc was telling him what he needed to hear. "So what can I do?"

"Go home or go hard."

"You mean go hard or go home?" Tyler asked, stating the famous quote.

"Exactly. Now about those payments..."

"Don't slip or trip. My insurance is paying for my visit with you," he told him.

"Good. Cause it's all about the Benjamins," Doc told him. "Now, about Nesha. I say you keep a close eye on her."

"You mean snoop?"

"I mean find out her daily routine. What time she wakes up. What time she goes to sleep. What time she pisses. If she jogs, I want you to follow her!"

"What about work?" Tyler wanted to know.

"Work comes first." He needs his money. "Find out if she's the girl that you fell in love with or the neighborhood hoe."

"Eh, Doc?" Tyler said with a frown on his face.

"It is what it is," he gestured with a shrug. "No matter how nice you put it, shit will always be shit, no matter what you call it. Go. Save your relationship," Doc pointed toward the door.

Boy, Tyler's situation is all fucked up, Doc examined. He didn't have that type of problem. Doc walked out of his office.

"Doc, where are you going?" his secretary asked.

"Out. Cancel all of my appointments," he requested and left.

CHAPTER 10 .

Tamra slid up and down on the gold pole with grace. She was doing good until she saw Anthony B and some of his boys walk into the club. She nearly broke her neck to get up off the pole and not let him see her. It was too late. He was walking her way.

She scooped up the money from her performance and hurried off the stage. She ran to the dressing room, hoping like hell he hadn't seen her. Needless to say, she didn't come back out of the dressing room until closing. As she walked to her car, she heard someone shouting out her name.

"Tamra," Anthony B called from his Lexus.

"Damn," she huffed. "What?" Out of all the people in the world, why did he have to know what it was I had been doing for a living? she asked herself as she opened her car door to get into her car.

Anthony B drove over to Tamra's car, "What's good. Why you didn't tell me you worked here?"

"Not something to go around bragging about," she said as

she got into her car.

"It is what it is," Anthony B stated. "You know you shouldn't be dancing, right?"

She rolled her eyes at the question. "And you shouldn't be selling drugs, but did I ever knock you?" she asked.

"Nah. And I don't knock you. All I'm saying is you could've come to me if you was having problems."

"I don't get down like my cousin," she chastised.

"I know. And that's one thing I respect about you. You do whatever it takes to make it. I like how you put it down."

"Put what down?" she raised a brow.

"That pole," he laughed.

"Stupid," she laughed along with him. "Don't tell anyone."

"Never. Real recognize real," he said to her.

"Yeah. I guess it does," she retorted.

"But, anyway, I best be on my way. I just thought I would get at you and tell you not to be ashamed about what you do. At the end of the day people going to be talking shit. But let them, while you get your paper," he drove off.

Anthony B was right when he said real recognized real. And she was recognizing that he was as real as they came. She just couldn't understand why her cousin Neatra didn't see it.

***

Neatra walked downstairs on purpose with a see-through lingerie set on. She pranced in the kitchen. Anthony B didn't even glance at her. She knew she had fucked up countless times. She just wanted him to pay her just a little bit of attention. She fixed a cup of orange juice. "Anthony B, you want anything to eat?"

"What are you cooking?"

"TV dinners."

"Hell no. Can you cook something else?" he asked.

"No," she answered.

"Damn," he uttered. What can this bitch do besides suck and fuck? he reflected in his mind.

"Yo. I have something for you to do," he commented.

Neatra strutted into the living room, "What is it?" she smiled flirtatiously.

"I need you to drive me to Florida next weekend. Think you can do that?"

"Yes. And when we get back you can take that restraining order off of me," she bent down and unbuckled his jeans. "Let me get some of this in my life," she rubbed his hard erection. Anthony B's head tilted back as Neatra took him into her mouth and started deep-throating him.

Anthony B knew he couldn't stay mad at Neatra for too long.

***

True to her word, Neatra drove Anthony B to Orlando, Florida and back. You know? Being the wifey type. Things were back to normal. She was stealing money out of his pants when she washed clothes, stealing out of his stashes he thought she knew nothing about. But she did, and she was ripping him off every chance she had.

She razzle-dazzled him with good head just to keep him in bliss. She was going on expensive shopping sprees, getting her hair and nails done, riding around in the brand-new Bentley with the chauffeur. Things couldn't have been any better. The more money men made, the more they started getting sloppy as hell. Neatra offered her stamp of approval. "I love Anthony B's dumb ass," she danced in the backseat of the Bentley.

CHAPTER 11

Nesha was tired of crying. She had decided that she needed to get out of the house. Earlier that day she had called her mother and asked her to keep Tyler Jr. She was shopping at the local T.J. Maxx when a lady asked her to help her find a couple of outfits in her price range. Without hesitation, she helped the elderly lady find three outfits, two blouses, stockings and high heels.

"Thank you," the lady smiled. "And here," she pulled out 40 dollars and gave it to Nesha.

"No, thanks. It's not always about money," Nesha replied.

"Thank you, honey. You should give this woman a job. She's the nicest lady I've ever met," the lady commented to the manager over at T.J. Maxx.

The manager responded, "She has to want to work here." He glanced at Nesha. "How 'bout it?" the lady asked Nesha.

Nesha's heart beat rapidly. It was almost as if she had peanut butter in her mouth. She heard the elderly lady speaking to her. "How about it, honey?"

"I don't know. I've never worked before," she answered truthfully, in spite of the awkward situation.

"Well, today might be your blessing," the lady said to Nesha.

"I could get someone to show you the ropes around here. So what's it going to be?" the manager inquired.

"Yes," Nesha smiled.

"Come on. I'll show you around and you can sign a few papers."

Nesha left the T.J. Maxx in her Acura. She turned up the music and started singing out, "I can feel the presence of the Lord. And I'm going to get my blessings."

She drove to Tyler's job to tell him the good news. "Can you tell me where Tyler Anderson is?" She asked the lady at the front desk.

She smiled, "And who are you?"

"His wife," Nesha commented.

"Oh. I didn't know he had a wife," the lady at the desk responded.

"Well, he does. So can you tell him I'm here?" Nesha spat.

"You tell him yourself. He's right over there," the lady at the desk pointed with her finger and smirked.

"Bitch," Nesha mumbled under her breath. She went over to where Tyler was. He was accompanied by nothing but ladies as he ate in the break room.

"Tyler, I made you some coffee," a girl named Brenda placed a cup in front of him.

"And I made you some apple pie," Katrina smiled, batting her eyes away at him.

"And here. You can have some of my leftover lasagna I made last night," Karin smiled and placed the plate of lasagna she had prepared for Tyler onto the table.

"Sure beats the hell out of peanut butter and jelly," Tyler

stated.

"Ewwwl," Karin cringed her face into a bunch. "I didn't want to say anything, but I notice you've been coming to work with peanut butter and jelly sandwiches every day." She smirked, "Men can't live off of peanut butter and jelly alone. What's up with your girl? She can't cook or something?"

Nesha placed her hand on her hips and commented, "Bitch, since you got all the answers, tell me why you all in my man's face?" Nesha put the girl in the spotlight since she wanted to be the center of attention.

"I..." she stuttered.

"That's what I thought. So shut the hell up. Tyler, I need to talk to you," she curled her nose up at the reckless hoe that was sprinkling salt on her name. "Heffa," she said in reference to the loose woman.

"Excuse me," Tyler stood up, embarrassed about the scene Nesha was causing, "Come on. Let me talk with you outside," he reached for Nesha's arm.

"Don't be trying to check me," she swung her arm out of his grasp, frowned and then followed Tyler out of the break room.

"What are you doing?" he growled.

"I should be asking you the same thing," she glared at the break room. "Got them bitches cooking you dinner and shit," she gasped.

He let out a deep sigh, "Answer my question."

"To come and see if you wanted to go out for lunch. I have some good news," she smiled at him.

Tyler huffed, "Can't."

"Why not?" she wanted answers.

"Have to go take some packages across town," he replied.

"What about later on today? Can you come by the house?"

"No can do."

"Why not? You haven't come to see me or your son..." she said before he cut her off.

"But I bring money every two weeks when I get paid!" he raised his voice in frustration. This woman had taken him through the most bullshit.

"It's not all about the money."

"Then what is it about?" he asked.

She cried, "Us. Our family."

"Don't start this shit again," he uttered.

"I love you," she poured her heart out to him.

"I have to go back to work. Miss me with that shit," Tyler stated.

Nesha wanted to go up in that break room and smack the shit out of him. But she didn't. She wiped her tears and left.

CHAPTER 12

Anthony B walked into the bedroom. As usual, Neatra was waiting up for him. "Hey, baby," she crawled on the bed toward him.

"What's good," he sat down at the foot of the bed.

"Nothing." She had just got off the phone with a guy in jail who she had been having phone sex with. He had her pussy wet, and she was extremely horny. "How was your day, baby?" she lifted his shirt.

"Stressful," he took a deep sigh.

"Let me see If I can help make it a little better. Let me help you out of those jeans," she unbuckled his pants and eased his jeans down, then tossed them to the floor so she could go into his pockets when he wasn't awake.

She shoved him back onto the bed. Made her way down to his nine inches or better. She tugged on his hard shaft and wrapped her lips around his stout cock. She began bobbing. Up and down.

"Oh, baby. That feels so good," he moaned. "Suck that shit, girl."

And that's exactly what she did. She sucked until the facial expression on his face said that he was about to bust. She moved as shit went sailing everywhere.

"Damn," Anthony B grunted. Shorty was no joke, he thought.

"It's not over," she straddled him and rode him like a wild woman.

Anthony B piped Neatra down like a jackhammer. Ram was the sound every time he pulled her down on his hard erection.

"Give it to me harder," she whined.

And that's what he did. He fucked her until her juices were flowing down his nut sack. "Was it the best you ever had?" she asked while kissing on his neck.

"Ain't no question."

"Good," she remarked. She watched him rol overl and go to sleep. She had dozed off too. She made sure to wake up the next morning bright and early. She got up and tiptoed out of the bed. She picked up Anthony B's pants and was about to go into them.

"What the fuck are you doing?" Anthony B asked with one eye closed and one open.

"Nothing," Neatra tossed his pants back to the floor.

"Bitch!" he flipped. "What the fuck was you doing?"

Neatra was scared as shit. She had got caught with her hands in the cookie jar. She had to think fast. "I was about to wash clothes," she lied.

"Bitch, toss my pants over here. I know you wasn't stealing from me," he raised his tone with her.

"No. You know I wouldn't steal from you. You must have some bitches' phone numbers in your pocket?" she frowned, using reverse psychology on him.

"Whatever, bitch. Let me catch your ass stealing from me," he told her. "Since when you wash clothes butt naked?"

"I do it all the time," she answered. "I'm a freak like that."

"Then bring your freaky ass over here and bless me this morning."

See, ladies, sometimes it pays to give your man some head every now and then, she thought to herself. Keep them happy, and they will keep you happy. She laughed as she took Anthony B's cucumber-sized erection in her mouth. He was happy, and she was happy, she thought as she slid the 400 dollars, she had stolen from Anthony B's pants under the mattress.

***

Malik, Anthony B's right-hand man and also his hired gun, sat across the table from Anthony B as they were eating at Hooters.

Malik laughed, "Yo. You alright, dawg?"

"Hell no," Anthony B scratched his scrotum. "I think one of these chicken heads I've been messing with gave me an STD."

Malik laughed his ass off, "You stupid, fool. Who was it?"

"I don't know. I've been fucking a couple bitches lately."

"Slut buckets, you mean," Malik shook his head from side to side. "When will you ever learn?"

"I was faithful until I started peeping shit out of the ordinary. But I need a favor," he told Malik.

"What is it this time?"

"I need you to go to the CVS and get me some shit for crabs, my G!"

"Early, my G!" Malik laughed. "Wifey going to kill you."

"She ain't going to find out, cause I'm going to get rid of the shit, early," replied Anthony B, scratching his nut sack at the same time.

"Check out the fleas on Fluffy," Malik teased.

"Enough with them sly remarks. Let's go."

"Early, my G, CVS. Early," Malik stated.

***

Neatra's cell was ringing. She looked at the screen and picked it up.

"What did I tell you about calling my phone, J-Kwon? I told you not to call my phone, and if I wanted to fuck with you, then I would call you," she snapped on him for being so stupid.

"I just called to say…" he paused.

She just hoped he didn't say no stupid shit like he loved her. She cut him off before he could say another word. "If you say you love me, you will not be getting anymore of this good pussy." I knew I shouldn't have given this tender-dick motherfucker no pussy, she pondered to herself.

"Hate to burst your bubble. But you a hoe, and don't nobody love you, but Anthony B," J-Kwon told her.

She laughed and knew he was right. "So what do you want?"

"Just to tell you I might've given you crabs."

"You what?" She raised her voice, "You stupid motherfucker!"

"You heard me, bitch! It ain't the first time you had fleas, and it damn sure won't be the last," he hung up.

"Oh shit," she mouthed. "This dirty-dick motherfucker done gave me crabs." She knew damn well better than to be fucking with J-Kwon's project ass. She had to think fast. Anthony B was going to kill her. What if she gave that shit to him? Come to think about it, she had been scratching down in her private region. She grabbed her handbag and headed out so she could go to the local clinic.

The whole time she was down at the clinic, she was cursing J-Kwon's ass out silently in her head. Project ass motherfucker. I'm never fucking with another thug out the projects again as long as I live! she promised. The doctor called her into his office, shut the door behind her and told her to be careful with who she was sleeping with and to stop having unprotected sex.

She wanted to smack the shit out of the doctor. But she didn't because he was exactly right. She drove home, thinking about what she was going to do. She knew Anthony B was going to come home and want sex. There was no way she was going to fuck him, knowing that J-Kwon had given her fleas. She could kill that fool.

What am I going to do? she wondered. She thought of a few things. J-Kwon had done her dirty and left her all alone to deal with her problems in the best way she knew. She could: one, be real and let Anthony B know — Hell no. X that out; two, sneak and put the cream the doctor had given her on Anthony B's private region while he was asleep. Shit. This shit is complicated. She realized that she should have never fucked with J-Kwon's local-never-gonna-make-it-project-ass-thug. She could kick herself for dealing with J-Kwon.

She had planned things out. She made it home and took a much-needed bath, placed the cream the doctor had given her on her vagina region, cursed in her mind at J-Kwon, got dressed, and waited for Anthony B to get home.

She made sure to wear loose-fitting clothes so Anthony wouldn't want sex. As soon as he came in, she rushed over to kiss him, "Hey, baby."

"What's up," he backed away as Neatra pressed up against him.

"Is something wrong?" she asked.

"No. Why would something be wrong?" he asked.

"I don't know. You just seem a little shaky. That's it," she commented.

"I'm good."

"You sure? Cause I can make you feel better. Sit down and let me suck you off," she grabbed his hand. She had to get some lice-killing shampoo on his ass before he found out she had given him crabs.

"I'm good, Ma. I'ma just chill tonight."

Damn, she cursed in her mind. "You sure?" she attempted again.

"Yeah, really sure." As bad as he wanted to fuck Neatra, the instructions on the medication he got Malik to pick up from CVS said not to have sex for ten days.

"Damn, baby," Neatra gave him a kiss and rubbed his plump dick, "let me break you off."

"No. I ain't trying to have sex tonight," he removed her hand from his private region. "Who said anything about sex? I'm on my period," she lied. "I just want to break you off."

"Nah. Cause then I'm going to want to have sex," he shot back, happy to hear that it was that time of the month.

"Just get some rest," he insisted.

"Where are you going?" she asked with her hands on her hips.

"Guest room. If I sleep in that room with you, you know it's going to be some good fucking. When do you come off the rag?"

"Three to five days."

That gave him a little time. "Holler at me then." He was about to leave, then remembered that it was time for him to make another trip to Florida.

He said to Neatra, "I need you to take me to Florida this week."

"Anything for you," she said, wiping the sweat from her forehead. That was close, Neatra thought.

***

Neatra called Tamra's cell. She had really done the dumbest shit in the world. She had driven to Tennessee to visit her ex-boyfriend Memphis on lockup. She had completely forgotten that she was supposed to be driving Anthony B to Florida in a few hours.

Damn, why isn't Tamra answering her phone? Just when she started getting impatient, Tamra answered. "Hello."

"Where are you at?" was the first thing Neatra asked. "Party or something?"

"What do you want, Neatra?" She was busy working at the club. "Why do you keep blowing up my line?"

"Cause I need you, desperately, for that matter."

"What do you need?"

"Well. I need you to drive Anthony B to Florida," Neatra replied.

"And why can't you do it?" Tamra asked.

"Cause I'm in Tennessee, visiting my ex."

"Memphis?" Tamra blurted out. "He's out?"

"No, not exactly," Neatra answered.

"You mean he's still locked up? You are going to see a thug that's locked up when you got a good man at home? You stupid. No, I won't do it," Tamra told Neatra.

"Hold up," Neatra pleaded. "I'll pay you."

Tamra was about to hang up until she heard about money. "How much?"

"Two grand."

"Where did you get that kind of money?" Tamra inquired.

"Stole it from Anthony B," she admitted.

"Trifling bitch," Tamra pondered. "You stupid. That boy goes out of his way to make sure you've got any and everything. And that's how you repay him?" she sympathized for Anthony.

"Hey, I'm the victim here. Don't act like if you were in my position you wouldn't be doing the same thing," Neatra declared.

"Can't say I would," Tamra clucked her teeth with her tongue.

"Well, you're a damn fool. But, anyway, make it 3,000, because as soon as you all get back, Anthony B will be so tired I can hit his pockets up and make my money back."

"Okay. I'll do it for three G's." But not for Neatra. Just to have the opportunity to be around Anthony B. "When is he planning on leaving?"

"Right now. You gotta hurry," Neatra suggested.

"Word. So when are you going to get back home?" Tamra asked. She had to go let her boss know that she would be leaving early.

"I might stay the whole weekend," Neatra told Tamra.

Tamra came to the conclusion. "You love this fool, don't you?"

"That's my dude. I just wish he wasn't locked up," Neatra smiled a gigantic smile.

"Stupid heffa," Tamra mumbled to herself, then said, "Enjoy your vacation."

"I will. Look, I really have to get going so I can check into this hotel," Neatra stated.

"Cool," Tamra replied. As much as I hate to admit it, Neatra has to be the dumbest bitch in captivity. Not only is she dealing with some petty fool doing a long bid, but she trusts me to drive her man all the way to Florida and not fuck him, Tamra smirked.

*****

Anthony B paced the living room in his basketball shorts and tank top, with a suitcase in hand. "Where the fuck is Neatra at?" he wondered. Sometimes I don't know whether to lover her or kill her dumb ass. She can't do shit right. Give a woman a castle and turn her into a princess, she will still want to only go no further than a hood rat, he pondered.

The doorbell raddled him out of his thoughts. Thinking it was Neatra, he snatched the door open.

"Hello," Tamra spoke. "You ready?"

"Ready for what?" he asked.

"Neatra told me to come and take you to FL," Tamra confirmed.

"What? Where is she?" he frowned.

"Look, don't get me into that. You want me to take you or

not?" she asked, scanning Anthony B's tall, well-sculptured body. He was too sexy for his own good. He was nearly 6 foot 2 and resembled the NBA guard Derrick Rose. Anthony B was light-skinned, with almond-brown eyes, short, groomed hair and kissable lips. The type of man that drove women out of their panties.

"Yeah, let's bounce," he suggested. "I have the keys already in the car."

They got into the Chevy Malibu and Tamra drove off. She noticed that Anthony B hadn't said a single word for the two hours they had been on the road.

"You okay?" she asked.

"Your cousin stupid," he uttered.

She didn't reply and kept driving. Her cell rang. Anthony B watched her as she answered. "Hey," she smiled. It was Mel, the guy she had met at the strip club. She could tell that Mel really liked her. He was begging her to spend some time with him. "Sorry, I'm busy this weekend. But maybe next weekend," she told him before she got off the phone.

"Who was that?" Anthony B asked.

"Why?"

"Cause I asked."

She smirked. "None of your business," she smarted off.

"Oh, it's like that?" he shot back.

"It is what it is," she commented.

He rolled up a blunt and lit it up. He turned up the music and relaxed as he caught an elegant high.

Oh no, he didn't, Tamra thought to herself as Anthony B fell asleep on her. She turned the radio to a smooth R&B station. "Oh God," she hollered out. "This is my song right here." She sang the lyrics to Alicia Keys' "I won't tell your secrets."

Word to life, Anthony B didn't know whether he was just high or Tamra was singing to him. But he was rock hard and trying his best to deny the fact that he was extremely enjoying Tamra's company. In the back of his mind he was thinking, Maybe Neatra's trying to set me up by sending her cousin Tamra to drive me to Florida. Be strong. Don't play yourself and look like a fool later, his conscience was telling him.

"I'm tired," Tamra yawned. "Why don't you drive or get a room?" she suggested.

"Pull over, I'll drive. Neatra already has me behind schedule." When Tamra pulled over, they switched seats. He drove while Tamra took a nap. He couldn't help but notice the short coochie cutters she had on and the way her breasts poked out from beneath her tiny top.

She was dead wrong for that. Look at them sexy lips and those hips, he thought as he drove. I wonder if she will run her mouth to her cousin if I touched that ass. He looked at her and got scared, then erased the thought. At last they were in Orlando, Florida. It took them nine hours, but they were finally here. He pulled into a Ramada Inn and tapped Tamra awake. "Yo. I need you to go get us a room."

"Where are we?" she glanced around.

"In Florida. Go get us two rooms," he told her. "This should be enough," he gave her close to 400. "Let me know if you need more," he told her.

"Be right back," she told him. She went into the front office and hollered at the clerk. She returned with only one room card. "Sorry to tell you the bad news, but they only had one double. So looks like we're going to be sharing a room." Not only did she save him some money, but she had made sure that she and Anthony B had to be in each other's presence for the night. "I hope that's cool," she checked.

"Fo'show," he said in response.

Tamra popped the trunk to the car and was about to grab her bags when Anthony B stopped her. "I got that."

She smiled. "Thanks. I'm going to get the door for you. You sure you don't need any help with the bags?"

"No. I'm fine," he stated.

You sure are, she silently admitted as she went to the room.

Anthony B sat the bags on the floor. "Yo. I'm about to roll and get something to eat."

"From where?"

"I don't know. But I do have a taste for some chicken."

"I heard the Popeye's chicken is really good," she informed him.

"See if I can find one," he told her and left.

Tamra was wondering what was taking Anthony B so long. He had been gone for close to an hour, so she decided to take a shower.

After finding some good weed to smoke, buying some blunts, then finding a Popeye's chicken, Anthony B returned to the Ramada Inn. As he walked into the room, Tamra was coming out of the bathroom with only a towel draped around her.

"Where you been?" she asked.

"It took me a minute to find Popeye's."

"Oh," she said. "Can you hand me that bag?" she asked.

"Yeah." He placed the food onto the table, picked the bag up and carried it over to Tamra. "What?" he asked her.

Tamra just glared at Anthony B and smiled, "Can I tell you something?"

"Fo'show."

"You promise to keep it on the hush?" she stated.

"Real recognizes real."

"I know." She let the towel fall to the floor. "And you look familiar." She kissed Anthony B. "I've been waiting so long for this," she proclaimed.

"Damn, girl." He cuffed her round ass with both hands and hiked her body so that her hands were gripped to his shoulders and her hips were wrapped around his buttocks region. "I wanna feel you inside me," she whispered into his ear.

"Damn, Ma." He slid his finger into Tamra. She thrust against it.

"You know we can't do this?"

"What?" She broke the kiss. "Don't tell me you're going to pass up on all of this." She went back to kissing him. "You see how wet it is?" She gyrated on his finger. "I want you." She kissed on his earlobe.

"I can't do this," he uttered out, thinking about the sexually transmitted disease he had. If it wasn't for the crabs, then it would've been a go!

"Then why are you doing it then?" she asked as he applied two fingers into her slit.

"Cause I'm stupid."

"I agree." He slid his fingers away from her.

"Cause all you needed was someone like me who would've been real with you." She turned and walked away.

"Tamra," he called as she went into the bathroom. "Can I talk to you?"

"You said all you needed to say," she let him know.

"Damn," he muttered.

Needless to say, Tamra had to admit that her entire trip to Orlando was truly a disappointment. She and Anthony B hadn't said anything to each other since last night, and they slept in different beds. She was still fuming about that whole ordeal. As she drove back home, her cell started going off. She answered, "Hello."

"Hello, beautiful."

"Hi, Mel."

Anthony B noticed the smile on Tamra's face and put the radio up.

"Can you turn that down, Anthony B? I'm trying to talk on the phone," she asked in annoyance.

"Hell no," he bobbed his head to the music.

"Asshole,"

"That makes two of us," Anthony B retorted.

"What you say?" she started arguing with him.

"If you hang up that phone, maybe you could hear," he said on the sly.

"Hey, Mel. Let me hit you right back."

"Is something wrong?" Mel asked.

"Yeah and no," she ended the call and smacked her tongue down, causing a clucking sound. She was curious to know, "What was that all about?"

"Who was that?" he wanted to know.

"Why?" she huffed a breath of frustration.

"Cause I don't want you talking to that fool when you around me."

"You not my man," she clarified.

"That doesn't mean that I like being ignored."

"You're not the only one," she said in reference to last night.

He felt he needed to save his face. "The mood wasn't right. When the time is right, I'll show you how real I keep it," he swore as he turned up the volume on the radio dial.

Tamra pulled up to Anthony B's place. "I'm so tired," she said as she parked out front. "Yo. Thanks a lot," he told her. "What do I owe you?"

"Truthfully?" she inquired.

"Truthfully."

She leaned over and tongue kissed him. She could tell he was really into the kiss. "Just promise to get at me when you ready to show me how real you keep it," she giggled.

He also laughed. "Fo'show. I better get in this house," he let her know.

CHAPTER 13

"Yo, man. I've been watching her and watching her and nothing is going on," Tyler said to his best friend Key.

Key took a sip of his gin and juice. They were at Skewers Bar in downtown Durham. "You gotta be the biggest fool in the world. I told you I saw her with some other guy. Some Tyler Perry looking motherfucker!"

"I don't care if I'm the biggest fool around. I'm going home to my wife," Tyler stood his ground.

"She must got some good snatch," Key muttered. Snatch is a code word men use referring to pussy!

"Wouldn't you like to know?"

"Tender dick motherfucker. Don't come back running to Key when you find out that your little princess ain't such a princess," Key said. "Don't say I didn't warn you!"

***

Tyler cut on his Kem CD and flicked the dial to his favorite tune, "There's nowhere to hide when loves is calling your name." He made his way to his apartment. He was tired of being Mr. Tough Guy. He was ready to work things out with Nesha for the sake of his son, Tyler Jr. "Hey, honey! I'm home," he yelled out.

God is not always there when you call, but He is always on time, Nesha thought as she got off from her knees after praying and ran downstairs.

"Baby," She leapt into Tyler's arms. "I missed you. Please say you won't leave us again." She wrapped her legs around him, fearful that he might leave.

"I promise, baby." He kissed her, palmed her backside and caressed it. "You know what I want?" He dug his finger into her slit.

"What's that?" She arched her back, giving him all of her.

"You." He leaned her back against the door and slowly undressed her until she was completely naked. A lovely sight. 36-35-40 was looking at him with a bird's eye view. "Make love to me," he ordered.

Nesha wasted no time undressing him. She unbuckled his belt, unfastened his pants, pulled his long rod out and began sucking him like her life depended on it.

"Damn, that feels so good." He wrapped his hand in her long tresses for support.

Seeing him about to buckle only made her pussy throb. She milked him down to the bone and had him panting. She played with her clitoris as she brought Tyler down to his knees.

"I'm coming!" He closed his eyes.

Good, she thought. She got up and grabbed his hand while he was still in La La Land. "Come on," she led him to their bedroom.

Tyler held onto the wall, still stunned from the good head. Damn, why had he stayed gone as long as he had? One thing for sure, and two things for certain. He is about to tear some pussy up.

Nesha got into the bedroom and stretched out on the bed in the doggystyle position. Tyler got right behind her and opened her up to insert her with his massive erection. He grabbed her hips, dipped into her and worked his hips with proficiency. Inhale, exhale. He moved in and out of her with deep hard strokes.

Nesha squeezed the pillow, "Yes, daddy!"

Tyler pounded Nesha down like a jackhammer, tearing the pussy up. "You like it rough, don't you?"

"Yes, baby," she managed to groan out, tits bouncing every way as Tyler smacked her ass with his hand. "Ouch," she hollered at the stinging sensation.

He turned her around to her side from out of the doggystyle position. How he did that? Nesha would never know. But she could feel all of him. He tucked her sideways as his dick smacked against her pussy lips like a car crash. "Ah, all," she complained from every jab to her stomach that he hit her with.

Tyler balled Nesha up like a pretzel where he dashed in and out of her until he could see her shudder. He continued to fuck her until he shot off his load.

Nesha curled up against Tyler, panting loudly. That was amazing, she had to admit. She was happy for once in her life, and God had answered her prayers. She had her man and family back together. Things can't get any better than this, so she thought.

***

"Yes, Doc. We're about to get married." Tyler rubbed his beard and thought about Nesha. "That snatch must be good," Doc asked.

"If I tell you, I might have to kill ya," Tyler teased. Or was he? He telling the truth?

"Well, Tyler, I'm happy for you. I hope everything works out," Doc Mel said to Tyler.

***

Tyler walked with a package into the front office of Century Real Estate. As he was walking, he saw Amber. Now, call him stupid, but he could never rid his mind of her. He erased those thoughts. Things were going too great with him and Nesha, and he didn't want to mess that up. "Hey, Tyler," Amber smiled at him.

"What's good," he spoke as he held a box in his arm.

"I didn't know you worked here."

"Yep. I've been working here for six years."

"So how is Nesha?"

"Good."

"And Tyler Jr?" she asked.

"Just great. Looking more like me every day."

Amber frowned. She felt sorry for Tyler. "You're really a great guy."

"Tell me about it," he answered with a slight grin on his face.

Amber wanted Tyler in the worst way. He had so many good qualities. "How about a cup of coffee?"

"Cool, I think I have a minute," he agreed.

"Right this way," She led him to her spacious office.

"Someone has it going on," Tyler mentioned.

She noticed him looking at her ass. "I know," she smirked. "Have a seat and relax. Sit that box down." She called for her assistant Bernice. "Can you go and grab us two cups of coffee and a couple of steak biscuits?" she ordered.

"Damn, girl. You have pull," Tyler told her as her assistant left the office.

She smiled, turned on the radio and moved to the sofa with Tyler. Damn, he was handsome, and smelling awfully delicious. "So, what have you been up too?" she gave him her undivided attention.

"Not much. You know, trying my best to stay above water. Thinking about getting another job. Things a little better now that Nesha's working. She finally got her shit together."

Amber couldn't believe it. "Nesha really stepped it up," she had to admit. "Oops," she covered her mouth. "That slipped."

He laughed. "I know. It surprised me as well."

"Yeah. That's good to hear. I can't remember Nesha ever working. That had to be your idea."

"Well, what can I say," he replied.

"I see someone has finally put their foot down!" She nudged him in his side.

"Yeah. Had to. You know, needed some help if I ever plan to get my trucking company."

"It'll work out," she reasoned with him.

Damn. I like those words. Too bad they are coming from someone else and not Nesha. "Nesha hates when I bring up that I want to do something else with my life instead of work for UPS."

"Who cares? You're the man, at the end of the day, and

she's supposed to be a part of your movement. Right behind you. If you decided to picket and protest, she's supposed to be right behind you with a picketing fence." She smiled sideways at Tyler, flirting a little, but smiling awfully hard.

He liked that smile. "You're cool."

"I know," she said with a grin across her face. "Now let me make sure you eat." She grabbed the complimentary foods from her assistant.

"He's cute," Berenice mouthed to her.

"I know," Amber silently mouthed back to her. "Make sure you keep yourself busy."

"You do the same," Bernice replied before looking at the nice gentleman and leaving. Tyler could tell that Amber's secretary was flirting with him. He smirked.

"She's a mess," Amber stated about Bernice.

"I see," he said as she handed him a sandwich and a cup of hot coffee. "So what do you do all day?" he asked.

"Try to get people to buy homes."

"Are you any good at it?"

She chuckled. "No, you're not trying to play me," she said out loud.

"Well," he shrugged. "Do you have skills or what?"

"Yes. And I have plaques to show it." She stood up and went to her dresser. "You see these?" she asked.

He got up to admire her prestigious awards. "Yes, I do. You're nice with it. Work with the kids, that's nice. Something I would like to do," he admitted.

"Well, you can. I'm at the Boys & Girls Club every Saturday from two to three in the afternoon. If you ever get time, feel free to stop by," she encouraged.

"Maybe I'll do that," he replied as he ate his sandwich and downed his coffee. "Yo, look. I really have to go. Can you get rid of this for me?" He left the cup on her desk. "Nice seeing you." He picked up the package, took the last bite of his sandwich, and just like that he was gone.

Amber took a deep sigh. Why did Nesha's conniving ass have all the luck? she pondered to herself. She should've been the one that should've been with Tyler, and not the other way around.

***

This dude Anthony B ass is going to be a problem, the specialist pondered to himself. That asshole was holding him back from the one thing he wanted so bad it didn't make any damn sense. He knew what he had to do. He hated to be a snitch, but who the hell cared? He got on the phone. "Hello, is this the police office?" he chuckled. "Yeah, I have one that will not comply. He's late on his payments, and he has skipped class like a young teenager." Doctor Mel laughed with a slight chuckle.

"What's his name?" the dispatcher asked.

"Anthony B." And the motherufcker is getting on my last nerve, Doc declared. "So hurry up and pick him up before he does any more damage." He couldn't have him messing up a for-sure thing, could he? He didn't want anything fucking up his date with Tamra that night. Don't drop the soap, motherfucker, he laughed out as he hung up. He remembered Tamra stating Anthony B's name on too many occasions. Not today, my boy. Tamra was all his.

After dinner and a movie, Mel and Tamra went to her

house for a little relaxation time. "Be right back," Tamra told him as he lay back on the bed. "I have to use the potty." She kissed him as he caressed her with his hands.

"Hurry back," he told her. His song was on. "I want you to dance for me so I can make it rain."

"Alright," she smiled. She could use the money. She could tell Mel was wide open. And after she fucked him, she was sure that the money, cars, clothes, and credit cards would come after. She went into the bathroom and applied on some smell-good that would blow his mind. She was smelling like peaches and cream when she walked out of the bathroom.

"Take them clothes off," he demanded as he stood up on the bed.

"Sit down. And don't touch," she shoved him.

"I want your hands in the air, like Buster Rhymes, so I can see," she said. Maybe she didn't have to fuck this lame just to get his money. There was no need to give her precious body away. She was saving it for a special someone.

She straddled Mel and thought about Anthony B. "Damn, you're rock hard," she replied as she swayed her hips.

"Got damn, girl." Mel's tongue hung out. "Let me try that out." He started flicking his tongue like a snake.

"No." She smacked his face.

"How much?" he wanted to know.

"Not enough. You can have it when I say the time is right." She smirked and knew it wouldn't be long until she was riding something foreign.

He begged, "Please."

"I don't like it when you beg." She grinded against him with her hips.

"I'll do anything."

"Anything?" she tossed him back onto the bed.

"Anything."

"Eat my pussy and I'll think about it," she spat.

"Please let me taste it," he begged.

She was about to sit on his face and let him blow air bubbles into her pussy when the phone rang. "Hold up. Keep that tongue out," she demanded.

She took the call. It was Neatra. She could hear that she was crying. "What is it?"

"They locked Anthony B up."

"Who locked Anthony B up?" Tamra inquired.

"The police. They just came and picked him up."

"For what?"

"That shit that happened not too long ago," Neatra answered.

"I thought that got thrown out." Tamra asked.

"No. He had to finish these classes, but he never did."

"What do you want me to do?" Tamra commented.

"To go with me to see what's going on," Neatra cried.

"Okay," Tamra smacked her teeth. She was worried about Anthony B as well. "I'll be there in a little while to pick you up," she said before ending the call.

"What is it, honey?" Mel asked as if he hadn't been eavesdropping.

"I have to go and take my cousin to the police station to bail out her boyfriend, or whatever." Tamra blew out a deep breath of air. "Too bad. Cause I was about to put it on you." She rubbed his face with her hand.

Damn. A brother couldn't hit the lottery to save his life,

Mel thought to himself.

Neatra and Tamra walked into the magistrate office, only to find out that Anthony B had no bond.

CHAPTER 14

Nesha was hard at work at her job at T.J. Maxx. Things with her and Tyler were all too well. She couldn't have been happier. She had everything a woman could ask for. She was getting the best dick in the world. She had a good job; had her own bank account and was even helping out with the bills. She had given her life to the Lord and was going to church every Sunday and Bible studies on Tuesdays. God had forgiven her for her squeaky past.

But D'angelo didn't forgive her. He walked up into T.J. Maxx like he owned the damn place. "Bitch, why ain't you been answering your phone?"

"Cause I'm engaged to be married, you piece of shit," she hurled at him, tossing up the hand so he could see the studded-out diamonds in her engagement ring.

"That chump done bought your raggedy ass a ring." That nigga was a fool if you asked him.

"What it look like? You going blind?" she asked.

"I don't like this shit," he commented.

"Well, deal with it," she said in annoyance.

"When we gonna spend a little time together?" He pulled her up against his body.

"Never." She turned her nose up to him and pushed him away.

"Never meaning not right now?" he answered.

"Never like as in never," she replied.

"You mean to tell me I ain't getting none of that good pussy?" he raised an eyebrow. She crossed her arms over her chest. "You're really a smart guy. I don't know why you never finished school," she frowned.

He pulled her up against him. "I need you, baby," he whispered in her ear. "I gotta have you."

"Too bad," she put some distance in between them. She couldn't see what she had seen in D'angelo. "You's a slug."

"What the fuck is that?" he looked around dumbfounded.

"You not too bright motherfucker. It means you ain't shit. A bum." She started naming all the no-good qualities he possessed. "A broke son-of-a-bitch. No job having, staying with his momma ass, crusty-toe ass nigga," she went on. "Never amount to shit ass motherfucker. Hotel staying, ashy ass, big frog-headed."

D'angelo had had about enough. He smacked the shit out of Nesha. "Bitch, your funky ass got some nerve."

"Is everything okay, Nesha?" Nesha's manager asked.

"This my woman. "Let's go," D'angelo answered.

"Yeah. I'm alright," Nesha lied, feeling like she was in another time zone. She definitely didn't want to piss D'angelo off anymore.

"Then bring your ass on," D'angelo grabbed Nesha by the

hand.

"Anybody else want some?" D'angelo asked, intimidating people as he walked through. "Nesha, where are you going?" her boss asked.

"I don't know," she said, before being slung and tossed in D'angelo's mother's car. D'angelo got into the car and turned the radio to his favorite tune. D'angelo's "I still love you, baby" played in the background.

What more could Nesha say? She was forced against her own will and taken to the nearest cheap motel. Some place called Save A Lot. "Damn, this pussy is good. You thought you could just leave me, bitch!" he dashed into her with deep strokes.

"You're hurting me," she yelled out.

"And you hurt me, bitch. Now you know how I feel." He continued to pump into her until he felt his body spasm.

***

Nesha tried to crawl underneath D'angelo's body as he slept like a baby. She had moved his arm, gotten up from the bed and grabbed her clothes.

D'angelo woke up out of his sleep. "You're going back home to that bitch-made motherfucker of yours?" he smirked.

She nodded her head, "Yes."

He grabbed her arm and pulled her to him. "Yeah, well when I need you, just make sure your ass picks up that phone. You hear me?" he shouted spit into her face.

She jumped. He put the fear of God in her. She nodded her head, "yes."

"Good bitch," he snapped.

As soon as he let her arm go, she dashed out of the cheap motel that smelled like beer, cigarettes and old box springs and hopped into the first taxi that passed through.

She didn't even bother to go pick up her car from work. She had a new problem on her hand. D'angelo. She hated she had ever given him the pussy. Anyways, maybe I could pay someone to take care of my problem for me. She started thinking of people who could do it. She needed money. Well, then again, I can always work something out. I can't screw this up. She was about to get married in a few months. She needed D'angelo out of her life for good. She paid the driver of the taxi and went into the house. Tyler was fast asleep. Good, she thought. She went upstairs to wash off the scum from D'angelo's slug ass off of her. She had to get ready for this mission, she was about to be on. She cleaned the disgust off of her, got dressed and caught a taxi to the hood in Chapel Hill, NC.

She paid the taxi fee and got out. She had found who she was looking for. A mean motherfucker named Chaos. "Chaos," she walked up to him.

"What?" he frowned, scratching his rough-looking beard. It was true, he hadn't shaved in over a month and a half.

"I need your help."

"What is it?" he asked.

"I need you to take care of a very bad man," she told Chaos.

"How much you got?"

"Two hundred."

"What you want me to do? Smack that mothefucker? Cause that ain't going to do nothing but make me go upside his head," Chaos laughed at his own joke.

"I need him dead." She thought about her son. Her engagement with Tyler. A woman had to do what a woman had to do.

"I usually charge at least five hundred if you want me to do it right," he negotiated. "I can make payments."

"Money up front or no deal," he let her know.

"I can write a check," she approached him cautiously to make sure no one could eavesdrop on their conversation.

"A killer once told me never have a written agreement. It might come back to bite you in the ass. Maybe you should come back when your money is right."

"No," she pleaded. "Maybe we can work something out?"

He raised an eyebrow. "Something like what?"

She walked up to him and nudged her arm into his private. "Maybe if you help me, I'll help you," she coaxed. "Big Fella."

He couldn't believe he was about to get it in with this good-looking woman here. "Right this way," he motioned behind the building in an alleyway.

"And hurry up. You do have condoms?" she asked as she hiked up her skirt.

"No, but I do have a grocery bag." He smiled his toothless smile.

"I think I got condoms in my purse." And thank God she had. She handed him a condom. He wasted no time plowing inside of her with his small ass dick. He was small but had endurance. He fucked her for nearly an hour before his endured ass finally bust a nut.

"Now will you do it or what?" she asked as he fell back against the wall.

"Shit. That pussy is good." He tried to keep his balance by

holding onto the wall. "Yeah. Who is it?"

She gave him D'angelo's info. His momma's crib and all, what kind of car he drove and places he frequently hung out at. She wrote him out a check for two thousand dollars. He grabbed her arm. "Don't worry about it, sweetie." He smiled and patted her on the ass. If he hadn't had such a little dick, she probably would've been back to get him to kill someone else. "You came to the right place," he assured her. "You come back, you hear?"

"Hopefully, if everything goes right, I won't have to," she said before she stepped off and hitched another taxi.

CHAPTER 15

Anthony B sat in his cell. He had to do sixty days in the county. To make shit worse, he hadn't heard shit from Neatra. But from what he was hearing around the cell block, Neatra was flossing his Bentley around and club-hopping. Shit probably wouldn't have bothered him if she would've come to visit him. But it had been over a month, and the only time he heard from her was when he had called, and she was at home. The bitch had been promising him that she would come and see him. "That bitch ain't shit," he muttered.

"Anthony B." The metal bars to his cell opened. "You have a visitor." He walked out of his cell and went to the visiting room. Maybe I was wrong about Neatra. He was dead wrong because Neatra wasn't sitting in the visiting room and waiting on him. It was her cousin Tamra.

See, that's what I like about this girl. She knows how to play her position, Anthony B thought.

Tamra smiled as Anthony B flopped down into the seat in front of her. She picked up the phone. So did he.

"What up, Ma."

"Worried about you?" she held her hand up against the glass.

"Real talk," he smiled. "You're looking good. Got these niggas gawking." He looked around the visiting room and noticed that the niggas weren't paying their girls any attention but were more focused on Tamra.

As if Tamra was reading Anthony B's mind, she remarked, "Tell them that this belongs to you." She giggled.

"You serious?"

She frowned, "Why wouldn't I be?"

"Damn, girl. Why you got that attitude?"

"You don't know," she glimpsed away and took a deep sigh.

It was visual that she was feeling Anthony B. And that's what he needed. Loyalty. "Yo, Ma," he told her. "It's me and you to the end."

She looked up and smiled. "You mean that?"

"Would I lie to you?"

"I don't know," she replied. "What about Neatra?"

"Tell her to get her shit out of my house when you see her."

"No. You're going to have to do that," Tamra half-chuckled.

"So, what have you been up to?" He browsed down at the keys in her hand. "Whose Lexus you driving?"

"Mine."

"I'm not even going to ask you how you got it," he stated as he leaned back in his chair. "Well, if you did, then I would've told you."

The reply he needed. "How?"

"This guy that I've been seeing," she responded.

"Did y'all fuck?"

"No. I can't believe you asked me that," she glanced at him

puzzledly.

"Well, who is he?"

"This counselor."

"Name?"

"This guy named Mel."

"Mel, who?" he inquired.

"Mel Brooks."

"Oh God," he covered his mouth and chuckled.

"What?" she replied.

"This punk motherfucker. He got me locked up because of you," he told her.

"I didn't have anything to do with it," she assured. "I would never do anything to hurt you."

"I can tell you serious about that, Ma. Do you remember talking about me to him? Cause that fool hates me."

She answered, "The one time when we were in Florida. You remember? The time when I told you to turn the radio down."

No. He couldn't remember. That shit what they said about women was true: They did have photographic memory. He had a confused look on his face.

"You remember? I was mad at you. I yelled out, 'Anthony B. I'm trying to talk on the phone,'" she tried to make him remember.

It came to him. "Yeah, now I remember. Look, does he treat you well?" he asked.

"He was," she flashed the keys to the Lexus. "But you know it's over now that I found out what happened."

"Nah. Let the games be played," he rubbed his hands together as he plotted his next move.

"What do you have in mind?"

"Let's milk this motherfucker for all that he is worth. You with me?"

"Yes, I'm with you," she answered. "And let me ask you this: If I do all of this, are you going to promise me that you will break things with Neatra and come get with me?" she questioned with serious intentions.

"I'm about to send her walking papers, as we speak," he told Tamra.

"So, I'll come back, and see you soon," she got up from her chair.

"Nah. We still have ten minutes left. Sit that ass down." When she sat back down, he said, "Now pull that blouse up and play with those tits for me. Tell me how you want it when I get hold to it."

"Anthony B, what if someone is looking?" she asked with caution.

"Show a little love to the men on lock up," he stated, leaning back and watching the show. Damn. I can't wait to get out so I can fuck the hell out of Tamra. Someone is going to get pregnant, he thought to himself as Tamra exposed her swollen nipples. He groped his dick. "Now play with that pussy for me," he encouraged.

"You are so freaky," she lifted up her skirt.

"You ain't seen shit yet," he declared. He was going to lick from her pussy to her asshole when he touched down.

***

Neatra went out to check the mailbox outside. She was expecting a letter from Memphis. Instead, she received a letter that would change her life up. It was from Anthony B.

"Look, Neatra. You just not keeping it real, so let's just both do each other a favor and go our separate ways. It was good while it lasted. Sincerely yours, Anthony B!"

"What?" Neatra asked as if she was the rap artist Lil Jon. She couldn't believe that Anthony B was calling it quits. Over her dead body, she thought. She went into the house to get dressed so she could take a trip to the jailhouse. She had on her "fuck me" heels, "forgive me" shirt and "baby, I'm sorry" skirt.

She entered the visiting room to see her boo. She took a seat on the cold metal chair and waited for Anthony B.

Anthony B took a seat, then picked up the phone. "You get your shit out of the house yet?"

"I'm not going anywhere." She held her hand up against the window and started crying. "Anthony B, you're all I have."

"Was," he corrected.

"Please. Don't do this. I don't know what I'll do without you."

"You better figure it out," he declared.

"Neatra looked up and saw J-Kwon waving at her from the cell block.

"Woah," Anthony B happened to look back. His male intuition told him something wasn't right. He glimpsed back at a nigga in his cell block. "You fucking that cat or something?"

She felt guilty and didn't know how to tell him that she had. She shook her head and wiped her tears. "No," she lied.

"You think I'm feeble-minded?" he barked.

"What's that?" she asked.

"Means stupid, bitch," he retorted.

"Anthony B."

"Anthony B," he mocked. "Get your raggedy ass up out of here, bitch," he slammed the phone, causing a scene. "Get the fuck up out of here," he yelled.

Neatra looked up and saw J-Kwon waving at her. She gave him the finger. Glad he was locked up.

***

Anthony B waited until the guards let everyone out and then approached J-Kwon, a low-life drug pusher. "Yeah, my G, let me holler at you," he spat to J-Kwon through clinched teeth.

"Ain't shit for us to talk about, homeboy. Everybody knows you a pussy. If it wasn't for Malik, cats would've been done robbed ya," J-Kwon started to chuckle at his comment. "And your bitch... I banged that bitch out more times than you, and you go with her?"

"Oh. You a crowd pleaser?" Anthony B snatched J-Kwon by his neck and started beating the shit out of him. "Rob me, mothefucker. Rob who?" he blanked out.

***

After beating the life out of J-Kwon and sending him to the prison infirmary with three broken ribs and a broken jaw, Anthony B reflected on his life in general. He knew deep down inside he had to do the unthinkable. Tried to turn a hoe into a housewife. That shit caused him time and also money. Her ass was through. He contemplated about Neatra and all the shit she had put him through. She had to go. Then there was Doc. This fool had got him locked up and hated on him in the worst way. And on top of all that, the fool was still charging him for taking those bullshit sessions. Maybe it was time to pay Doc a visit.

Nah, he had another plan for his bitch ass. Anthony B rubbed the strings of his beard underneath his chin. Payback is a bitch. Believe that. He laid back on his bunk and started plotting on ways to get back at all of the cruddy individuals in his life.

***

D'angelo slept on the couch at his momma's house. He was tired as shit. He had been out three days partying, drinking, smoking a little but not too much crack. His socks had holes in them. He stank and hadn't taken a bath since his three-day adventure of getting high.

He felt a smack on his cheek and moaned, getting mad. His mom knew not to fuck with him when he had been out on the prowl. "Get the fuck on and leave me alone, dammit," he spat.

"Wake up, motherfucker," a voice lingered.

"D'angelo thought it was a dream, until he felt what felt like a dick in his mouth, but only it wasn't a dick. It was cold steel. He woke up and thought he was in prison and someone was trying him. He started swinging, knocked the gunman on his ass, got up and connected with his head once, twice, three times, four, and another, etc. He beat the motherfucker until he dropped the gun and pleaded for his life. "Who sent you?" D'angelo slapped him like a bitch.

The gunman was dazed and felt like he was in the ring with Iron Mike Tyson in his prime. This motherfucker has some big hands. He squinted his eyes as a fist rammed into his cranium.

"Who sent you?" Dangelo asked again. "You want to live, don't you?" He picked up the gun.

"Please. It was some girl. She sent me here," he whined like a little baby.

Nesha, D'angelo thought. "How did she look?"

"Pretty. Light skin," Chaos stuttered for his life.

"Nesha," he frowned and couldn't believe that bitch had sent a hit man to his mother's house out of all places. "I'ma kill that hoe," he uttered. "Right after I kill you," he told the hired gun. "You shouldn't have taken on the job, you fool." Bang! Bang! Bang! was the sound of the gun. Good thing mom isn't home. He cleaned up with bleach and Ajax and dragged the body outside in a Hefty trash bag.

He asleep, he thought to himself as he tossed the body into the dumpster. "On to the next one," he uttered.

Nesha was vacuuming her house when she heard screeching tires. She ignored it and thought someone was just showing off their new ride. She saw Tyler Jr. in his rocking chair and smiled: the only man she loved in this cold world other than Tyler. She heard a loud bang and turned her focus on the door.

"Bitch, open up."

Her heart nearly jumped out of her chest. "Oh shit!" she mouthed. Her legs went limp. She didn't know what to do. She had cement feet and stood motionless.

"Bitch, open this door." D'angelo crashed into the door and fell on his ass. "Damn." He got back up and shook off his dizziness. He needed more force. He backed up a hundred yards and charged the door.

Nesha thought fast. She slid the sofa up against the door, then the flat screen behind it, the wall unit, fridge, washer. She had that super woman force when it came to her life. She was scared to death. She could hear the loud ram into the door. She jumped and was about to run when she remembered Tyler Jr. was in his rocking chair. She ran back to get him and then ran upstairs in search of a place to hide.

D'angelo was nearly unconscious, trying to get into the house. By the time he got the door open, he could see the cartoon character Tweety Bird flying around his head, singing and chirping and shit. His body ached. He let out a loud moan. I'ma kill this bitch for making me climb all this shit. And who helped her move all of this furniture? A moving company? He was in search of Nesha, so he could wring her neck and watch her slowly die. He checked everywhere.

The closets, the kitchen, bathroom. Then rechecked everything again. He even checked the windows to make sure she hadn't hopped out of one of them. Damn! He was about to go when he realized he had missed a room. He cracked the door open.

Nesha lay up under the bed like a carpet. Word to life, she didn't even breathe. She panicked. Her heart was beating like a drum when she saw D'angelo's sandals. His feet smelled so fucking bad that she nearly wanted to comment. His feet were right in front of her, making her want to cry. To make things worse, he just stood in front of the bed and right in front of her.

Nesha turned her head as D'angelo tortured her with his feet.

"Damn. Where is this bitch?" he asked out loud. He passed gas. Really fucked up the place. Picked his nose and tossed the boogers on the bed.

Nasty motherfucker, Nesha cringed from the smell. She wanted to barf. That shit was strong enough to make a grown man cry… or a baby.

"What the fuck was that?" D'angelo glanced around. He could've sworn he heard a baby cry.

Nesha placed her hand over Tyler Jr.'s mouth as her heart

thumped.

"Bitch." D'angelo pulled Nesha from under the bed. Child and all.

"Don't hurt me," she begged.

"Bitch." He pressed his finger up to her head. "Now I'm about to kick your narrow black ass." He was about to smack the living daylights out of her when she held her son in front of her.

He stopped. "Get your ass up. You're going with me," D'angelo explained, not even wanting to look at Nesha.

Nesha gave a sigh of relief. She knew D'angelo really loved her in spite of the fact that she loved Tyler. She also knew that deep down inside she woul also loved D'angelo. She had never stopped loving his no-good ass. They had a special bond that was inseparable.

***

I should've let D'angelo kill me. It's been nearly a month, and I'm laid up in a cheap motel called Save a Lot. I'm being held against my will. Kidnapped by this no-good, no job having, no money having, broke ass, stinking motherfucker. I knew I should've never given this boy this fire! Pussy!!! I always knew it would come back to haunt me. I think about Tyler. And how I fucked up his life. I often pray to God and ask Him to help me get as far as possible from this slug ass piece of a man who has made my life a living hell. But he hasn't answered my call. And D'angelo, well, he's using me for his own convenience. He hops on top of me, pumping my body with his stinking sent. I hear the baby cry.

"Shut the fuck up," D'angelo barks. "Lil bastard," he has the nerve to say. "Give me this good pussy," he moans.

And like a dumbass I start gyrating my hips despite of the loud hollering from Tyler Jr. Dear Father in Heaven, please forgive us, for we know not what we do. "Damn, that feels so good." She gripped D'angelo's ass cheeks as he drove deep inside her thighs, and deeper, deeper until he hit rock bottom.

**

Got some good and bad news today. The good news is that I might have some idea where Nesha and Tyler Jr. may be. After filing a missing person's report, to no avail, and searching high and low for my son and my future wife, my best friend Key hits me with the ultimate bombshell. Tells me he saw the guy that looked like Tyler Perry and followed him to a nearby motel that he thought Nesha may be in.

Key had a real street mentality and wanted to go blazing into the motel. But I told him to stay put until I got there. So here I was. I took a deep sigh as I pulled into the Save A Lot motel. Key was already out of the car with what I could see was a gun in hand. I just hoped we wouldn't have to use it, Tyler pondered as he got out of the car.

"What are you waiting for?" Key asked with the gun in his hand. He was ready to kick some ass. "Let's go," he announced to Tyler. "That bitch gotta be in the motel with this bamma," Key led the way.

"Why would you think that?" Tyler followed.

"Because that woman was never any damn good. I just hoped you would figure it out," Key replied.

"Not Nesha." She wouldn't do me like this. She wouldn't

leave me for a month straight worrying about her and Tyler Jr., Tyler thought.

"All this shit this bitch took you through. I'ma kill this motherfucker she up in here with," Key assured as they upped the steps.

"Don't go overboard," Tyler told Key. "Let's find out what's going on first..."

"Good. Cause we're here," Key stated.

"Is that Tyler Jr.?" Tyler questioned. "My son!" He took a step back, rammed into the door and knocked the shit off the hinges.

To Be Continued

Epilogue

Nesha had a bunch of loose ends she had to fix before Anthony B returned from his stint in jail. She had already told a few college and street niggas to stop calling her phone because she didn't want shit affecting her relationship with Anthony B. He would be home soon, and she had to throw out all of her dirty laundry. Lord only knew all the skeletons she had in her closet. She got out of the taxi. She had flown out to Tennessee for one reason, and one reason only. She paid the taxi and got out. Pulled the tiny string she called a thong out of her large backside and walked up to the large jail house in downtown Memphis. She took a deep sigh. She really didn't want to do this, but she knew she had to.

She showed her identification card and went into the visitation room. She was with a bunch of other girls who were also faithfully visiting their men on lockup. No homegirl didn't come up her wearing those busted ass pants. Oh no, she doesn't have the nerve to act like that's her real hair, when she knows she has on a wig. Oh no, she didn't come up here like that, that bitch is out of pocket. If it had been her, she would've never been caught with cheap nails, fake Gucci bag, fake outfit and

Payless Jordan's.

And what about this bitch with all these Bay-Bay kids? Look like the old woman in the shoe with so many kids she didn't know what to do. She was so busy turning her nose up at this girl that she nearly jumped when Memphis finally walked up. She grabbed her heart. "Damn. You scared me."

"What's wrong, sugar?" He kissed her lips and took a seat beside her. Before he gave her a chance to answer, he complimented her, "You sure look nice."

And he wasn't lying. She was wearing a short mini dress made by Prada and long-wedged heels that made her appear taller than the 5 foot 6 she actually was. She blushed from the compliment. Not too hard because she knew she had to cut ties with Memphis.

"What's wrong, baby?" he questioned. "You haven't said one word since you arrived." She took a deep sigh, then came out and said, "Because I can't come up here and see you again."

Memphis contorted his face into a snarl. "What? Bitch!" were his exact words. He thought maybe he hadn't heard her right.

"You heard me," she retorted before she heard what sounded like a gunshot. She went deaf. She didn't realize what happened until everyone turned their focus on her. Memphis had smacked the dog shit out of her. She was about to apologize, "I'm so..."

Before she could finish her statement, Memphis grabbed her up by her neck. "You mine, bitch. You ain't leaving until I say you leaving," he choked the living shit out of her.

She was on her tiptoes, dangling in the air, trying to call for help, but it was as if no one could hear her half-mumbles.

"Bitch, I'll kill you," Memphis shook and choked her at the

same time. "Until Death does us part!"

"Don't kill me," he pleaded as she fought to save her life.

"You killing me if you plan on leaving me, bitch." He was snatched up by the guards. He broke free and managed to smack the shit out of Neatra before being restrained just to let her know he wasn't playing with her. He yelled out, "I'm serious. I will kill you, bitch."

Memphis was kicking and screaming wildly as he was being escorted from the visiting room. "We got history, bitch. I taught you how to suck a dick," he took pride in saying.

Neatra was sobbing on the floor. She could see all the blank stares people placed upon her. Memphis didn't have to make that statement about her sucking dick, although it was the truth.

She grabbed her aching face. She was so sick of these project ass men. She promised herself that she wasn't spreading her legs for no one but Anthony B, just as long as she lived.

"That was some tacky shit," smirked the girl with the fake nails, fake Gucci bag, fake outfit and Payless Jordan's that Neatra had been clowning. "She could have at least had the audacity to send that niggga a Dear John letter. But no, she wanted to come up here thinking she was Michelle Obama, when you ain't shit but a project hoe out of the ghetto. Some bitches have no class." The girl with the fake nails, fake Gucci bag, fake outfit and Payless Jordan's shook her head at Neatra in ignorance. "You can take a bitch out the projects, but you can't take the project out of the thot."

Neatra could hear everyone in the visiting room laughing at her because of this bum bitch with the Payless Jordan's. She got off of her sore ass and held her head high.

Neatra knew the girl wearing all the knock off was only

hating because she was rocking some shit that hoe had never seen or heard and probably couldn't spell. Neatra figured, these bitches today were fucking for free, unlike her who needed money! "Step your fuck game up and find a man who will get you out them Payless shoes, cow," Neatra uttered out indirectly.

She laughed all the way out of the jailhouse and into her taxi that she had flagged down. Don't blame me because I ain't sitting in the projects, sipping lemonade with y'all bitches talking about how broke we are, she smirked. Project. Who them bitches calling project? With they raggedy asses. She clucked her tongue. Them bitches ain't about to go to no house that's paid for, go on no shopping sprees like they crazy, ride around in the Bentley with the chauffeur all day, sip Chardonnay, Dom P, Moet, Sex on the Beach at the club. They can't make it rain on sexy male exotic dancers with they niggas' drug money like I could, she smirked.

She needed to cut it out. Another one of the bad habits, she picked up while Anthony B was locked in the slammers. Damn, she missed him. She couldn't wait until he was home. Although he was tripping the last time she had gone to visit him, she knew all she had to do was give him some bomb head to get rid of his frustration. As far as she could see, niggas in jail had a lot of frustration built up inside of them. She remembered the smack-down she received from Memphis. She took a deep sigh. She never meant to hurt him. He just needed to understand that he was locked up. And what did he expect? That I was going to wait three years for him when I could be getting some dick? He got me fucked up, she snickered and then laughed out loud.

We Help You Self-Publish Your Book

Made in the USA
Columbia, SC
27 September 2024